I0666374

Timmy and the Evil Dr. Vonvellicator

First Edition

Published by The Nazca Plains Corporation
Las Vegas, Nevada
2007

ISBN: 978-1-934625-42-2

Published by

The Nazca Plains Corporation ®
4640 Paradise Rd, Suite 141
Las Vegas NV 89109-8000

PUBLISHER'S NOTE
Timmy and the Evil Dr. Vonvellicator is a work of fiction created wholly by *Christopher Trevor's* imagination. All characters are fictional and any resemblance to any persons living or deceased is purely by accident. No portion of this book reflects any real person or events.

Cover, Fleshblack Images
Art Director, Blake Stephens

Dedication

My buddy Adam, for fiendish inspiration and endless support...

Timmy and the Evil Dr. Vonvellicator

First Edition

Christopher Trevor

Contents

Introduction for Timmy and the Evil Dr. Vonvellicator   9

Timmy meets and is de-feeted by Dr. Von Vellicator   11

A Bet with Reggie   31

Timmy Backman meets Christopher Trevor and Vince (maybe)   53

Timmy's Sensitive Man Nips (The Day after The Fundraiser)   115

The Bound and Gagged Dishwasher Boy   143

About the Author   165

Introduction for
Timmy and the Evil Dr. Vonvellicator

It seems I never tire of tricking and tickling my good buddy Timmy Backman. He is forever finding himself balanced perilously on a ticklish ledge or in yet another ticklish predicament. Whether it's his good buddy Ronald holding the poor Timmy Backman tickle captive yet again at his tickle palace, a place safely hidden away in a remote area somewhere in upstate New York or his brother Bruce tricking him, its always ecstasy to hear Timmy sing his song of laughter. Or perhaps his loving wife's best friend Valerie once again tricking the handsome and ticklish guy into the device known as "The Spinning Chinaman" and spinning Timmy round and round and tickling him in between. And then of course how can any of us forget Bull the bartender and his leather CO-horts in "Timmy at The Leather Bar" when poor Timmy's plans to teach a cocky friend of his a lesson in humility turned out to be yet another tickle lesson for our tickle hero/victim...

Now, in this latest installment of tickle tales we find others wanting to, or somehow being led to by fate in getting in on the tickling action of Timmy Backman. A Japanese businessman is introduced, a man fascinated by Timmy Backman after having met him at a most unusual fundraiser event...an event that will for now remain a mystery. Sir Leekalot, the Japanese businessman manages to swing a deal with Timmy's vice president at his place of work and Timmy finds himself being edged and worked over in a teasing and sexual manner...in his own office at his place of work...

In "Timmy Backman meets Christopher Trevor and Vince (maybe)" the author himself, his buddy Vince and a new diabolical character (eerily named Ronald) are the villains this time out for the ticklish Southern gentleman. This story also has one of the author's cliffhanger and nerve-wrangling endings...leaving readers wanting more and wondering what will become of their tickle hero/victim now.

Timmy's friend Reggie challenges Timmy to a sinister wager and gullible as ever Timmy accepts and then an evil doctor manages to snag Timmy in his clutches when the reserve soldier comes for a routine inspection of the doctor's facilities. In this story we learn that Timmy still serves Uncle Sam every other week or so...and even in that capacity he manages to wind up as a tickle victim...

As always, "Happy Reading" and Best Wishes from: Christopher Trevor

Timmy meets and is de-feeted by Dr. Von Vellicator

Author's Note: Here is yet another ticklish tale for your reading pleasure in the ongoing ticklish trials of my tickle hero and star, Timmy Backman. As was quickly noted in my tickle novel, "Timmy's Ticklish Trials" Timmy Backman spent a few of his younger years in Uncle Sam's army, a handsome and ticklish soldier boy. Now, as the years have marched on Timmy is employed as banker/lawyer, but as is revealed in this story he also donates some time as a reserve soldier to the army every month. With that in mind I found that that is a good way to keep the ticklish boy in uniform. In this story the reserve soldier is sent on a routine assignment by his unseen CO, Officer Jeff Masters, to investigate the inventions of a certain Professor Von Vellicator, (Vellicator as I learned means "ticklish" in German) a man who has done many projects for the government over the years. The assignment, which to Timmy Backman seems as routine as any other he has been sent on in the past goes awry for the Soldier boy when the professor so cleverly captures him and subjects him to still more ticklish trials... It is explained briefly within the story how Timmy wound up captured for tickle torture yet again, but I felt that it made more sense to simply get to the meat and potatoes of the story by beginning it where the poor soldier has already been captured and is tethered to a tabletop, his feet dangling off the end of the table and within easy reach for the fiendish professor. Recently I introduced the real Timmy to an old friend of mine named Shanna, a lovely young lady that I had the pleasure of working with over the years. I was astounded to learn that Shanna, like Timmy has a very kinky nature, so with that in mind I placed her in the story as the sly receptionist who lured Timmy to his latest ticklish demise. She also secretly lusts for the handsome reserve soldier so it stands to reason that she might be back in a future tickle tale to have the ticklish Timmy Backman in her clutches and all to herself. So, with all that in mind and said I offer you my latest tickle tale starring my wonderful ticklish buddy, "Timmy Backman…"

The Story:

"Ya vole Soldier boy Bayckman," the German Professor Von Vellicator said to his captured prize, handsome army reserve soldier Timmy Backman as he studied the soldier's paperwork that had been in his attaché case. "I vill be wiz you shortly, een the meantime just lay zere and be comfy…as you Americans call it…hee, hee, hee… Vor now I need to look over yer papervork to see joost vhy your superior's vould have sent you here meddling."

The paperwork had not been for the professor's eyes to see, but once managing to snag the investigative (meddling) reserve soldier Professor Von Vellicator was pretty much able to do whatever he damn well pleased. As the professor looked over the paperwork his brows furrowed and with a sinister looking expression on his face he glanced repeatedly over at the haplessly captured reserve soldier. The man was extraordinarily handsome; nearly six feet tall, because of his height he nearly didn't make it to fit atop the table he was presently stretched out on, on his back, his patent leather shoed feet nearly dangling off the end of said table. Handsome beyond anything the professor had ever seen before, beautiful shiny green eyes, salt and pepper colored hair that obviously had been a dirty blond years ago, a rugged square jaw ala Dick Tracy and even in his dark green colored uniform complete with a two inch black stripe down each pants leg, a pale green long sleeved shirt and black tie it could be seen that the reserve soldier was in tip-top muscular shape. The way his huge chest, bowling ball sized biceps and sinewy triceps pressed against his uniform jacket was a delight to see as he struggled while tethered to the tabletop. Obviously this reserve soldier boy worked out on a regular basis. He wore a wedding band too, making him even more of a fine capture the professor thought fiendishly. He wondered how this reserve soldier's wife would react seeing her strong and handsome hero of a husband in the position he presently was. Each time the professor glanced over at Timmy as he laid there the reserve soldier's heart thundered in fear in his chest.

"Ah mine soldier boy Bayckman, my veeeery sweet soldier indeed, hee, hee, hee, from vhat I am zeeing een your papervork here I can awnestly zay zat you shood neyver have meddled in avvairs of moment," the professor stated as he sat a few feet away from the table that Timmy Backman was tethered to. "But now zat I have you een a much secured position I am sure vee vill get to zee bottom of zis you and I, yes?"

"Yes? No Professor Von Vellicator, *no* way Sir!" Timmy grunted in his sexy Southern accent, his head lifted up off the table and him yanking helplessly at the iron shackles secured around his wrists and ankles that held him fast to the table as he lay on his back atop the structure, his muscular arms at his sides. "What you have done in capturing and restraining a United States reserve soldier is totally against the law! Professor, *this is* unacceptable..."

"I shall decide joost vhat is acceptable unt not Soldier boy Bayckman..." the professor stated, stood up and stepped to the foot of Timmy's table. "Vhat ees not acceptable ees you showing up here, surprising me with your probing, snooping inquiries and expecting me and mine staff to cater to your vhims...and all joost because you come here in your hayndsome looking uniform..."

As the doctor spoke he trailed the fingertips of one hand over the toes section of one of Timmy's patent leather lace-up military style shoes as his feet dangled off the end of the table.

"Uniform is right Professor Von Vellicator, and *this* uniform I'm wearing proves that I'm here on official government business Sir," Timmy blabbered angrily. "This isn't me in my business attire, oh no Sir! Two weeks out of every month I donate my time as an army reserve soldier and you and your lab are the assignment my CO assigned me. When he finds out what you've done in capturing and restraining me you'll be in deep trouble Sir!"

"OOO, I sciously doubt that mein handsome heir," the professor chuckled and to Timmy's shock he leaned down and planted a few delicate but deliberate kisses across the toes section of Timmy's patent leather shoe that he had moments ago just been fingering. "Because I am sure that you, as a soldier boy knows that you being captured by me means that you have bungled your mission, as you Americans vill call it...hee, hee, hee mein soldier boy, and I do mean mine. I do have you after all...*I have you...* and because you have bungled your mission, because I have in capturing you, burned you zo to speak, your CO will mete out I am sure what you Americans call, harsh deescipleen..."

"Discipline you mean, oh my word..." Timmy grunted and lay his head down.

As Timmy lay there trapped and shackled the professor kissed and licked the toes section of his other patent leather shoe. The captured soldier had to wonder why the nutty professor (no pun intended where the movie title is concerned) was so transfixed on not just his paperwork that he had confiscated but also on his military shoes. Timmy knew that his CO, Officer Jeff Masters would no doubt tan his naked ass for this bungling. The captured solider had seen the old fashioned sort of discipline dished out upon his buddies in the reserves in the past. JEEZ...soldiers spanked like they were little kids, hard nosed warriors, true combatants over Officer Jeff Masters knees no less...JEEZ... Army reserve soldier Timmy Backman knew, "HE KNEW" that he had to find some way out of this latest predicament he found himself in... His CO had sent him here on a most routine mission, to gather information about the reports that the government had been receiving about the eccentric Professor Von Vellicator and the inventions he had been supposedly working on. The professor was well known when it came to inventions. He had even invented a few gizmos that the United States government had purchased, so it stood to reason that they would be interested to know why the man was being so secretive with his latest creations. From what Timmy Backman knew the professor had not returned any phone calls, he had not responded to any e-mails or regular letters in the mail where his inventions this time around were concerned. When Timmy asked his CO why he had chosen him for this assignment the reserve soldier was shocked to hear it when Officer Jeff Masters said, "Your buddy Ronald Greene recommended you for this. Mr. Greene and the professor knew each other way back it seems. He said you have lots of experience when it comes to inventors and their machines." So without another word and with a hard gulp of shock Timmy accepted the mission and proceeded to the address he had been given for the professor's lab...a place on the other side of town, a place very far out of reach. And upon his arrival the professor captured the uniformed tickle hero...with a little help of course...

"Professor Von Vellicator, you cannot be looking at my paperwork," Timmy bantered through clenched teeth as the professor resumed perusing the reserve soldier's top secret documents. "All of that is confidential information...that I had in my danged attaché case..."

As Timmy prattled on and on he glanced over at his attaché case as it lay strewn on the floor beside his uniform hat.

"Dang it all..." Timmy seethed and again struggled fruitlessly in his metal bonds.

The image of Professor Von Vellicator fingering his shoe and then leaning down to plant kisses on it sped through the captured reserve soldier's mind. He did not want to give life to the thought that followed that one. If the professor was transfixed with his shoes then it stood to reason he would more than likely be transfixed by his socks. And if he was transfixed by the captured soldier's socks then he would most DEFINITELY be transfixed by Timmy's bare feet...no, better not to go there Timmy thought, trying desperately to put it out of his mind that the professor had been licking and kissing his patent leather lace-ups.

"So, as you Americans say Soldier boy Bayckman, it would appear that the tables, they have been turned on you, yes?" the professor teased Timmy as he stepped to the head of the table, forcing Timmy to arch his head back a bit now so that he had to look up to see the professor as he loomed over him.

"Yes...NO...Professor Von Vellicator, you must release me now, the table turning on me has gone far enough Sir," Timmy prattled, his head arched back.

"Not quite far enough mein soldier," the professor chuckled, grabbed an end of the table and gave it a hard push.

Suddenly, the table that Timmy was secured to was spinning round and round...

"OH shit, oh my word," Timmy cried out as he spun round and round.

When the table stopped rotating the professor gave it another good push, harder this time.

"OH MY WORD of words," Timmy bantered, lifting his head up and down and looking across at his stretched out torso as he spun and spun. "I feel like I'm fastened to a danged old fashioned record player."

As Timmy spun round and round he saw the professor still looking over his paperwork.

"So you and Meester Ronald Greene know of each other no?" the professor asked his prize as the table stopped spinning.

"Uh, yes, you could say that I have the unfortunate luck of knowing Mr. Ronald Greene," Timmy replied somewhat miserably as he tried to get his bearings after having been spun on what he now knew was some kind of rotary tabletop.

Thoughts of Ronald and what he put Timmy through in the past flitted through the captured reserve soldier's mind. He quickly pushed the thoughts away as the professor put down the paperwork and stepped again to the foot of the table that Timmy was fastened to.

"Professor, please, tell me at least, what in hell do you plan on doing with me?" Timmy asked as Von Vellicator began unlacing one of his patent leather military style shoes.

"Does thees answer your question my sweet soldier Bayckman?" the professor inquired and Timmy's thoughts reeled.

"OH NO, no, Professor, don't, DO NOT take my shoes off my feet Sir," Timmy demanded loudly, struggling mightily now in the bondage.

"But Soldier boy Bayckman, you are een noooo poseeshon to stop me, yes? NO..." the professor teased.

"Yes...I mean, no, I mean, yes, YES, you must stop this, you must release me!" Timmy pleaded, struggling mightily; the reserve soldier feeling totally despaired at having been duped upon his arrival at the laboratory and captured.

"So you vere sent here to invaystigate my laboratory and my eenventions eh mein Soldier boy Bayckman," the professor said and once Timmy's first patent leather shoe had been unlaced the man began slowly prying it from the reserve soldier's foot.

Timmy's heart hammered in his chest in mortal fear as his black socked foot was exposed.

"Oh my word, NO, no, Professor Von Vellicator, what are you doing Sir?" Timmy grunted throatily and wiggled his toes under his sock as the musty scent of his nylon dress sock mixed with shoe leather wafted through the air.

Ignoring the restrained reserve soldier's pleas the professor dropped Timmy's shoe to the floor, it landed with a CLUNK and he quickly got busy unlacing Timmy's other shoe. As he worked slowly and methodically at getting Timmy's second shoe off his foot he said, "Now tell me Soldier Bayckman, why on earth, as you Americans say, hee, hee, hee, why would your government be so veeery eenterested in me, hmmm?" As the professor spoke he slowly got Timmy's other shoe off his foot. Once more the scent of sweaty nylon sock and musty shoe leather wafted through the air. Timmy felt his cock churning in his uniform trousers as his balls seemed to shift in their sac. He licked his dried lips and thought of how he had once again been had...by his so called buddy Ronald Greene of all people. And this time Ronald was having someone else do his dirty work for him.

"Professor, you have to understand Sir," Timmy said as his other shoe hit the floor and he looked down at his black socked feet as they lay propped and restrained at the end of the table he lay on. "The government always, ALWAYS does routine checks and investigations on people in the news who are working on something new, especially something like what you've been dithering with. And you did not respond to our inquiries Sir! OH my word, give me back my shoes and release me Sir!"

"Perhaps your government is theenking my inventions are somehow harmful, yes?" the professor asked, wrapping his hands around one of Timmy's socked feet and leaning down towards it, sniffing as he went.

At this point Timmy pursed his lips in anger and through clenched teeth stated, "Professor Von Vellicator, the government doesn't think anything of your inventions, how could they? I haven't handed in my report yet..."

"Und you vill nawt be haynding een any report whatsoever Soldier Bayckman," the professor replied and pressed his thumbs hard against the bottoms of Timmy's black socked foot.

"OH MY WORD and just exactly what is that supposed to mean Professor?" Timmy asked in a pleading tone of voice.

The professor seemed to know just where to press to find Timmy's sensitive pressure points because the captured reserve soldier felt very tingling sensations coursing through his feet and up his calves. The professor pressed harder against the meaty bottoms of Timmy's socked foot.

"Professor, I am a government official, and again, I am wearing a uniform to prove it," Timmy repeated his earlier litany. "And YOU WILL do well to re-shoe my feet and release me Sir!"

"Yes, yes, you are vearing a uniform, but you seem to have lost your shoes yes Soldier boy Bayckman?" the professor teased his conquest.

"YES, no, I mean, uh, no, I have not lost my shoes," Timmy replied, his head spinning a bit as the doctor continued caressing his foot, sending shockwaves of chills through him.

"Und I vill do vell to teach you Soldier boy Bayckman to not, to NEEVER soobject me or my laboratory to surprise vessits, yes? NO!" the professor said angrily and leaned down further and slithered his tongue across Timmy's socked toes.

"OHHHHHH, YES, I mean, no...I mean..." Timmy said, chuckling a bit as he said it.

"Ah mine soldier, nothing is more relaxing for a man than to haave his shoes removed, yes?" the professor asked and moved to Timmy's other foot, quickly gripping it tight with two hands, pressing his thumbs against the bottom of it, massaging it in a tickly manner.

"No...no..." Timmy said in a guttural sounding tone of voice, his hands clenched into fists at his sides, knowing all too well what he was soon to suffer.

The reserve soldier could hear the laughter now...HIS...

"But don't you mean yes Soldier boy Bayckman?" the professor teased sadistically. "Hee, hee, hee..."

"Yes...yes...it's relaxing, but no, no...sometimes it can be peril... no..." Timmy went on and on.

"OOOOO my dear soldier boy, your socks are a beet musty, hee, hee, hee," the doctor teased his prize and leaned down to slither his tongue over Timmy's toes as he had done with his other foot.

Timmy lifted his head up off the table and laughed a bit as he said, "No, no, I mean, yes, my socks are a tad musty there Professor, but leave my danged feet alone in my socks huh?"

"Yes, yes, no, no, vhat ees thees a vord game Soldier boy Bayckman?" the doctor chuckled.

"Please don't do that," Timmy stated emphatically.

"Oh my hayndsome soldier, soon you vill sing high C's for me, count on eet," Professor Von Vellicator said, wiggling Timmy's big toe through his sock.

"H-high C? NO, NO, no..." Timmy gasped.

"Tell me Soldier Bayckman, are your socks always so moosty and scented or are you just veeery nervous here with me today?"

"Yes...no...yes..." Timmy panted. "Oh my word, I don't know what I'm saying anymore here..."

"I vould theeenk Soldier Bayckman, that some of my special therrrapy ees in order vor you, as of...NOW, ya vole?" the professor asked and let go of Timmy's foot.

He stepped to the head of the table and seductively loosened Timmy's tie a bit for him.

"Wh-what are you doing now Professor?" Timmy asked as he gathered his thoughts. "L-leave my danged tie alone Sir! And I demand that you re-shoe my feet..."

"Vee do not vant you choking vehn you beegeen your song for me Soldier boy Bayckman, yes? NO!" the professor laughed as he unbuttoned the first button of Timmy's shirt after having loosened his tie.

"I don't sing Professor," Timmy reeled.

"Troost me, you vill seeng like a canary veeery sooon mein soldier," the professor quipped and playfully tugged Timmy's loosened tie.

Smiling evilly the doctor stepped back to Timmy's socked feet...

"Sing...sing...canary...no, oh no," Timmy said in anguish as the professor took up position at his trapped feet and held up his long finger-nailed hands.

The professor strummed his fingernails from the bottoms of Timmy's heels up to his soles, his toes and then back down again.

"Oh NO NO NO NO, HAHAHAHAHAHAHAHA, you nutty Professor!" Timmy squabbled crazily. "I knew it; I just knew you would tickle my danged feet... HAR, HAR, HAR, HAR, HAR, HAR!"

"Und joost as I said mein soldier, like a canary you will zing, er, sing, now lets see eef I can make you sing higher notes, yes?" the professor chuckled and flicked his dexterous fingers harder and faster against the bottoms of Timmy's trapped socked feet.

As the professor glided his fingernails up, up, up, the bottoms of

Timmy's feet, from his heels to the balls of his feet to his toes the sounds of the metal shackles and chains attached to them at Timmy's ankles and wrists made clanking noises. He struggled fruitlessly in the bondage as the professor continued tickling him finger-wise...

"HAHAHAHAHAHAHAHAHAHAHA!" Timmy shrieked louder now as the professor squeezed one of his feet tight and tickle tortured the bottom of the other one at the same time. "OH DANG it all, what a combination this is, massage therapy mixed with ticklish devilish torture, OOOOOOOOOO, HEEEEE, HEE, HEE, HEE, HEE!"

Timmy's head bounced up and down on the soft tabletop, he hee, hee, heed as he watched the professor move his hands faster and faster it seemed over his black nylon socked feet...

Now, az zoon az I hayv varmed you up, az you Americans so quaintly put it, I shall demonstrate one of my eenventions that you zo nosy, nosy, nosy came here to eenvestigate, yes Soldier Bayckman?" the professor quipped from the end of the table.

"OH MY, HAHAHAHAHAHAHAHAHAHAHA! WHAT have I fallen into this time?" Timmy screamed through his laughter. "Inventions, I was sent here to investigate inventions...they have to be tickly things...somehow I should have known it, HAHA! OH WOE IS ME..."

"Az zee zong zays Soldier boy Bayckman, zing, zing a zong," the professor teased his captured prize meanly. "Zing for a zong of teekle torture mine soldier boy, zing for me mine angel of laughter..."

"HAHAHAHAHAHAHAHAHAHAHAHAHAHAHAHA!" Timmy screamed as the professor pressed his fingernails hard, harder, and harder against the meaty bottoms of his black socked feet.

Timmy sang as the professor had requested as he trailed those fingers at what seemed like warp speed up and down poor Timmy's feet. Poor Timmy though did not think he was singing, he was helplessly laughing his fool head off. Timmy's feet wriggled in the restraints and he was by then sweating in his uniform as he lay trapped atop the table...

"PL-please, please Professor Von Vellicator, please STOP, stop tickling me Sir! OOOOOOOO, HEEE, HEEE, HEEE, HEEE, HEEE!" Timmy pleaded as his head spun now. "OH MY WORD, HAHAHAHAHAHAHAHAHAHA!"

"But ov course solider boy Bayckman, but only for a short time I assure you," the professor stated, stopped tickling Timmy's feet, gave the table a push to set it spinning a few times and stepped away from the still laughing soldier for a moment. "I vould naut vant to deprive you of experiencing my eenventions virst hand...

"Or in my case, first foot you might say huh?" Timmy cackled as the table rotated.

"Veery cleverly put Soldier boy Bayckman," the professor replied and when he stepped back over to the table he stopped it spinning and glared down at his ticklish treasure.

Timmy looked up and saw that the professor was holding a spray can...

The ticklish guy gulped hard.

"My virst machine is joost down zee hall mine teeklish soldier," the professor said and aimed the nozzle of the spray can at Timmy's nose and mouth.

"OH NO!" Timmy railed as the doctor pushed the plunger down on the spray can.

Timmy was not fast enough to hold his breath as the stinking contents of the spray can invaded his nostrils. He inhaled the rancid odor and found himself in a very sleepy state, a stupor of sorts...

"OHHHHHHHH..." Timmy moaned as his head lay back atop the table.

He felt the shackles on his wrists and ankles being undone but could do nothing to defend himself as horror of horrors, he felt his uniform being slowly stripped off him...beginning with his belt being undone...

As he was unclothed he heard the professor chuckling a bit...

"S-stop, oh my word, d-don't..." Timmy groaned, mustering what strength he had.

But to the reserve soldier's dismay the professor sprayed his nose with another dose of whatever the spray can contained. Timmy groaned loudly and was then deeper in the stupor...

A Short While Later...

"Dang it all, oh my word, what's the point of THIS now?" Timmy asked miserably, his head still spinning from the effects of the gas he had inhaled as he was led out of the room where he had previously been shackled to a table in his army uniform.

To his utter consternation the reserve soldier now found himself stripped of his uniform down to his tight fitting white kangaroo pouch style briefs, his calf length black nylon dress socks and as humiliating as it seemed his army cap was perched on his head. With his hands roped tightly behind him and a black silk blindfold tied over his eyes the captured Timmy found himself being led down what he thought was a hallway, an uncarpeted hallway at that, as the cool feeling of linoleum under his thin socked feet attested to.

"Right thees vay mien soldier," Timmy heard Professor Von Vellicator saying as the man held tightly to the reserve soldier's forearms, just above where the mounds of rope were plied round and round his crossed wrists behind him. "I vill be zo happy to zhow you one of my eengenious eenventions. Just step zlowly und you vill do vine, er, fine. Mine English as you can tell ees not all eet shood be, yes Soldier Bayckman?"

"NO, no Professor, never mind your danged English, OH MY, I'm nearly naked here and I get the feeling you have me in public view," Timmy bantered in a near panic as he was slowly and carefully led along.

The reserve soldier's cock was fear hard in his white briefs and he could feel the tip of it peeking out of the fly opening, and to add to his kinky misery his cock was dribbling pre cum.

"WH-what's with stripping me you crazy professor? I'm a reserve soldier, you can't do that to me, but then again, oh my, you did do it, put me in LA LA land and stripped me down to my shorts and socks," Timmy recited and shook his head a bit. "Got my danged hat on me huh? A soldier's hat does not a uniform make Professor! And what's with the danged blindfold huh? OH NOW this is all too much here..."

"You are oondressed zo zat you vill be more comfy," the professor said and reached down to steal a squeeze on one of Timmy's melon shaped ass globes. "And zee blindfold is zimply to make it a BEEG zurprize for you, yes?"

"More comfy for what pray tell?" the reserve soldier asked in his Southern accent.

"WHY, vor my eenvention vhen you are, how do you Americans say, vhen you are tethered to it, yes, zat ees eet, vhen you are tethered to it," the professor quipped and again squeezed Timmy's ass globe. "Zere, mine English vas rather goot just then, yes?"

As the doctor chuckled and moved poor Timmy along Timmy could only grimace miserably behind his blindfold...

But it was when Timmy heard the professor's receptionist's sweet sounding voice when his jaw dropped and his mouth inched open in shock.

"Good afternoon Professor Von Vellicator," Timmy heard Shanna, the receptionist say snidely.

"Good God, I really am on display here," Timmy whispered in disbelief at the sound of the receptionist's voice as she greeted her employer.

Timmy involuntarily jutted his muscular chest outwards and hunched his shoulders back nervously.

"Und goot afternoon to you mine Shanna," the professor said and halted Timmy in his step.

Timmy recalled meeting the receptionist upon his arrival at the professor's lab. It seemed so long ago now. He also quickly surmised that she was part of the ploy in capturing him. He seemed to recall her having offered him a "refreshment" sort of drink while he waited to see the professor. He also recalled the lusty look in her eyes when she first looked up and saw him standing there so statuesque and handsome in his uniform, his hat clamped under his arm, total respect to have removed his hat when in the presence of a lady.

"And good afternoon to you as well Mr. Backman, or was it Captain Backman?" Shanna asked, sounding just as snide.

"It's Major Backman," Timmy said, a look of anger on his blindfolded face. "And may I say that from the look of things you Miss are in just as much trouble as the good professor here. You obviously aided him in capturing me..."

As he spoke Timmy's cock grew stiffer and peeked further out from the fly opening of his tight fitting kangaroo pouch under shorts. Shanna smiled as droplets of pre cum oozed from Timmy's cock slit. Like a lot of men Timmy grew hard in the cock when he was feeling fear.

"And may I say Major that you look extremely sexy in just your underpants, socks and hat," Shanna giggled. "I especially like that medal you have pinned on the side of your underpants..."

"OH MY! Such desecration," Timmy shouted thoughts of one of

his jacket medals pinned to his under shorts beyond humiliating.

Timmy recalled the receptionist being beautiful, with dark olive complexioned skin, shiny black shoulder length hair and dark, dark sexy eyes. She was dressed plainly in a skirt and blouse, but she was seductive nonetheless Timmy remembered a bit more. He also remembered how well endowed she was in the area of her ample bosoms, all day nursing he would think he could do on her big tits.

"I vill be demonstrayting for zee soldier my eenvention een room vour," the professor said to Shanna. "Please zee to eet that vee ees noot deesturbed at all..."

"Yes Sir Professor," Timmy heard Shanna say. "I do hope you will enjoy the demonstration Major Backman..."

As the professor and Shanna laughed fiendishly, looking at each other in a conspiratorial manner the professor tweaked one of Timmy's very pronounced nipples. As he did so Timmy's visible cock head leaked more pre cum. Shanna licked her lips hungrily as the professor brought the soldier into "Room Four."

"Unt here vee are," the professor said happily and clapped his hands together after closing and locking the door to the room he had brought Timmy into.

He quickly took the uniform hat off Timmy's head and placed it on a chair that was in the room.

"Now, before I remove zee blindfold I vill position you just zo," the professor said and stood Timmy a few scant inches from one of the most diabolical machines he would ever see.

As Timmy stood wherever the hell it was that the professor had balanced him he could still feel his head spinning a bit from the doses of gas he had been treated to earlier...

"DANG, what is all this?" Timmy asked no one in particular. "I was sent here on a routine assignment...and look at me now...captured, tied, blindfolded and de-uniformed, MY WORD!"

Standing beside his captive now the professor proceeded to whip the blindfold off Timmy. The reserve soldier allowed his eyes to adjust back to the light and then he took in the sight of two things in front of him...

"OH my word..." Timmy said and his cock pounded fear hard as it more than peeked out of his under shorts at that point, his testicles in his under shorts seemed to swivel around in their sac. "OH NO, you all can't be serious here Professor..."

What Timmy saw firstly was a short wooden board with straps attached to it. The board was pressed atop a wooden structure wheel-like device of sorts... He saw how a man would fit right well atop the wooden board...

Timmy took a few steps back on his socked feet but could not take his eyes off the electronic gizmo that was set up in front of the wooden structure that he knew all too well that he would soon be lying on and strapped down to... The electronic device looked like something out of a science fiction tale. It was a LARGE square device mounted atop a metal wheel-away. At the moment it was locked firmly in place however, and the crème de la crème of the electronic gizmo, a long rod with a cone-shaped fuzzy device tethered to the end of it mocked Timmy.

The reserve soldier duly noted that the long rod with the fuzzy device at the end of it was actually a spindle...it would spin, just as the table that Timmy had been tethered to earlier had spun, just as his head was still spinning, the rod and the fuzzy cone shaped device would spin...

As Timmy looked intently at the fuzzy device his memory wreaked havoc on him and he said the name "Ronald" followed by saying "My ticklish trials..."

"Ya, ya, your teeklish trials," Professor Von Vellicator said with a grin as he stood next to Timmy, a scissor in hand. "Zoon ve shall zee joost how veery teeklish your leetle perineum is, yes mien soldier boy?"

"OH TARNATION, you have got to be kidding me here Professor," Timmy squealed, looking at the professor's devilish inventions. "You mean to tell me you plan to tickle my asshole...WITH THAT?"

Timmy hunched his shoulders up again in a nervous fashion as the professor began snipping his underpants off him.

"H-hey, what all are you doing now?" Timmy asked.

"Vell now, lets be reasonable shall ve Soldier Bayckman?" the professor asked, sounding as if Timmy had just asked the dumbest of questions as he continued snipping away Timmy's under shorts. "I can noot possibly teekle your rosebud back there if you are wearing these pesky under zhorts now can I?"

"OH dang, at least I had 'em on while you had me in the hallway,"

Timmy said despondently as his underpants fell off him in tatters.

The medal that the professor has pinned to Timmy's underpants fell to the floor as said underpants were snipped and snipped. A few moments went by as the professor seemed to revel in the task as he slowly snipped away Timmy's underpants. When the last of them were snipped off Timmy's erection pointed straight up at the ceiling, it oozed thick droplets of pre cum and his balls dangled low between his thighs... The professor seemed to be drooling at the sight of Timmy's thick pulsing manhood.

The reserve soldier gasped breathlessly as the professor took him by his upper arms, said, "Thees vay Soldier boy Bayckman..." and moved him on his socked feet toward the wooden structure...

"oh my word..." Timmy said huskily as the professor propped him onto the wooden board on his back, his long legs dangling down at first.

Timmy watched in dread as the doctor lifted his legs by his socked ankles, lashed his feet spread wide to the ends of the board and then positioned the fuzzy cone shaped device on the rod by aiming it directly at Timmy's gaping and exposed shit chute...

With a look of total terror in his eyes Timmy nearly blanched when the professor snapped on a pair of tight fitting gloves.

With his hands lashed behind him and still swooning a bit from the gas he had inhaled earlier Timmy was virtually helpless to stop the doctor from doing whatever he wanted to him...and what he did was liberally grease up Timmy's asshole and ass walls with a jelly based lubricant. Each time the doctor's latex gloved fingers entered him rectally Timmy's cock twitched and dribbled pre cum...

"Unt avay ve go mine heir," the professor whooped a few moments later and threw a control lever to the upward position on the electronic gizmo.

"WWWWWHHHOOOOOOOO!" Timmy found himself screaming seconds later as the fuzzy whirly thing began doing its black magic. "HAAAAAAAAAA!"

The cone shaped device slithered its way spinning round and round into Timmy's most private crevice... The reserve soldier felt totally and literally invaded back there as the thing nestled inside him as it went...

Poor Timmy squirmed like a fish out of water on the wooden board as the fuzzy cone shaped device spun its way deeper into his slimed anal canal, tickling the daylights out of him as it went, round and round and round…

"AAAARRRHHH, HAHAHAHAHAHAHA! OH MY!" Timmy keened loudly, his head spinning like he was in orbit now. "S-STOP this thing, oh you nutty professor! HAAAAAAAA!"

As Timmy laughed he clenched his bound hands into fists and tears streamed from his eyes…

"AAAAYYYYYYYYY! Y-you all can't do this to me Pr-pr-Professor Von Vellicator!" Timmy ranted crazily. "I am a danged reserve soldier, HAHAHAHA, m-my superiors will hear of this! OOOOOOOOOHHHHHHHH HAHAHAHAHAAHA! Oh for fuck's sake, y-you're ticklin' or to be more precise here, your devilish invention is tickling my danged asshole! HAHAHAHAHAHAHAHA!"

Timmy rocked from side to side in an attempt to force the invasive spinning device from his anal hole. Instead it seemed that it burrowed its way deeper inside him…making his eyes cross in his head. From his teary eyed vision Timmy saw the professor making notes on a legal pad. But it was what the professor's receptionist did when she entered the room that really got Timmy screaming…

"NO, NO, NOT THAT, oh my word!" Timmy laughed. "HAHAHAHAHAHAHAHA, n-not that lady!"

"Say it like you mean it Major Backman," Shanna said as she videotaped Timmy's latest ticklish trials. "That erection you have there tells me how much you're enjoying Professor Von Vellicator's invention."

She moved closer to Timmy and filmed him as he laughed and laughed and laughed…

"NO, y-you can't be filming me lady," Timmy pleaded. "HAHAHAHAHAHAHA!"

Then, as he lay there laughing and as the fuzzy device spun and tickled his hole Timmy shot his load all over himself. Shanna and the professor laughed along now with their captive as Timmy ejaculated without his huge cock having been touched at all… As the fuzzy device did its work Timmy laughed and let loose with yet another jet stream of jazz. By the time he was done jazzing he was splattered all over his face and upper body with thick creamy white man juices.

"OHHHHHHHH! TH-this is too much now!" Timmy panted

and shot off a last dribble of cum.

The ticklish reserve soldier slipped into a stupor and heard himself laughing as if from far, far away...

When Timmy came to a short while later he found himself back in the original room where Professor Von Vellicator had had him earlier... He groaned a little as he woke up and when he realized he was not tethered to the table he sat up a bit on his elbows...

"Oh my," he grunted as he looked down at himself, still clad in just his danged black socks, not even his torn underpants on him now.

"Vell, vell mein heir, and how are you veeling Soldier Bayckman?" the professor said as he sidled up next to the table. "And joost exactly what deed you theenk of my whirly whirler?"

"Well, that's about as good a name for it as any I would say," Timmy replied sarcastically as he lay there, his body matted with man sweat and caked up and dried cum, his cock semi erect and slimy looking between his legs. "Tickling a poor guy's asshole has to be the height of depravity you crazy professor...but seeing as you had your lovely receptionist film my peril looks like you got it over on me now..."

The professor smiled wickedly down at Timmy... Timmy squirmed atop the table as the feelings of tingling still enveloped him in his asshole. He took a deep breath as the professor stood next to him as he laid there, his head still swooning.

"You vill seemply haynd in a written report based on your findings here, yes Soldier Bayckman?" the professor asked the muscular god-like reserve soldier atop the table.

Timmy nodded despondently, knowing that if he reported what the professor had done to him that he would simply hand over the incriminating video to Timmy's superior, Officer Jeff Masters.

"Goot, I am glad ve have an oonderstanding," the professor said and tweaked one of Timmy's nipples. "But before you leave there are steel the vindmills you must experience mein soldier boy..."

"H-HUH?" Timmy asked and sat up further on his elbows. "WH-what windmills are those Professor? What in tarnation do you mean experience them?"

"Vell now mien soldier, I am zure zat you vant to zee more than joost one of my eenventions," the professor said, grinning down lecherously at the naked but for his black socks reserve soldier. "Eet ees vhat you came here vor after all, YES?"

"YES? NO!" Timmy panted. "I came here on a routine assignment and what I got instead is unforgivable, so if its all the same to you I'll simply get dressed and be on my way Professor Von Vellica---"

But before Timmy could finish his sentence the doctor quickly held up the spray can and pointed it at Timmy's nose and mouth. Timmy did not have a chance as the doctor quickly pushed the plunger down and dosed the reserve soldier...

"OHHHHHHHH!" Timmy whimpered and fell back atop the table...once more in a stupor...

When he came to about twenty minutes later Timmy saw that he was again shackled to the tabletop, but only at the wrists at his sides. His feet had been bared at this point, his black socks nowhere to be seen. When he lifted his head up and looked across at himself he saw that his bare feet were locked in and encased in two heavy-duty plastic boxes...

His feet were slightly elevated in the boxes and when he saw the small windmills with the feathers attached to each spindle in the boxes he began laughing involuntarily...

"Vhy mien soldier boy Bayckman I have noot even started the vindmills spin, spin, spinning unt you are laughing already," the professor said, sounding confused.

"WH-why waste time?" Timmy laughed louder. "OH WOE IS ME....HAHAHAHAHAHAHAHAHAHAHAHAHA!"

A few seconds later the windmills within the boxes were spinning their feathers against Timmy's bare tootsies. In the boxes Timmy's feet danced and flopped around as they were tickled. From the side of the table the lovely Shanna was again filming her and Dr. Von Vellicator's unwitting and unwilling ticklish star...

A Bet with Reggie

Note from author Christopher Trevor: I have known Timmy Backman now for a few years. He is truly the best tickle buddy I have ever known. Let it be known I adore the guy, from his salt and pepper colored hair, to his charming Southern accent (I love phone chatting with him his voice sends me over the edge), his oversized nipples, what he and I call his man tits and all the way down to his soft and ultra-tickle sensitive black socked feet. Over time I and this wonderful gentleman have spun countless tickle tales and even had two books published, "Timmy's Ticklish Trials" and "Timmy and The Hong Kong Tailor." Within the stories in those books Timmy has been tickled by an array of villains, and when captured by these villains it usually is the ticklish guy's own fault. The handsome laddy seems to have a penchant for getting himself into tickle trouble. Timmy walks a thin line between loving and hating being tied and tickled. The huge and muscular Ronald is Timmy's so called buddy who obsessed over and eventually abducted Timmy in the middle of the night, right from his own home and spirited him away for three days of endless tickle torture. Valerie is the sexy athletically built woman with the legs and feet of a dancer, who feeds Timmy's most erotic desires, she is also his most heated nemesis when it comes to his wife's attentions. Valerie has on numerous occasions tricked the ticklish Timmy Backman into her sadistic spinning wheel invention, known as "The Spinning Chinaman."

Bull is the ruggedly handsome bartender from the leather bar who not only had the tables turn on Timmy at the leather bar and had the handsome Southern guy tickle tortured there...but also at a business fundraiser where Bull captured Timmy and made him the main ingredient in a huge salad. Timmy's prank playing brother Bruce is usually at the heart (and sole) of these ticklish predicaments that the ticklish laddy finds himself in. In real life, Tickle Master Vince and myself, author Christopher Trevor love tormenting Timmy with our fiendish tickle plans for him. And now, with all that in mind, after just naming but a few of Timmy's tickle tormentors, "Timmy Backman" gives us yet another villain to add to the mix, Reggie. Reggie, a handsome Asian tickler who will tease and coax Timmy into a wager...a wager to see if the ticklish handsome laddy can hold his juices... or perhaps to be tickled into losing his juices..., That said, we give you the latest installment in Timmy's ticklish trials, "A Bet With Reggie."

Happy Reading,

Christopher Trevor

How did I get myself into another predicament like this? Oh my word, how did I manage to let Reggie talk me into this...this danged bet... this wager? And pray tell, how did I think that I would ever have a chance to win? If you've read my past history you know that I always have a streak of luck...all bad when it comes to things such as this.

It all started with the friendly banter between Reggie and me. He's always teasing me about how he will strip and tickle me...and to add to that he says he will make me all sexed up, get me hard in the crotch...*and even make me cum*. Can you imagine that? Make me cum, of all things. And I'm always giggling and going along with him. Oh, woe is me.

Then finally one day I said, "Reggie, your Asian princess might be able to make me cum, but you could NEVER make me cum...not against my will." I was emphatic.

Reggie's eyes sparkled, "Timmy, are you offering me a challenge?" He grinned and licked his lips.

"Uh, well not exactly," I stammered as I got a little nervous. Yes, it did indeed sound like a challenge I was presenting.

"Well, it sounds like a challenge to me," Reggie grinned at me and playfully tugged at my tie. "And I'm up for the challenge. I bet I can make you cum...and I can overcum your will. Hee, hee buddy. So Timmy, you're not chicken are you? You're not scared that little ole Reggie could actually make you cum? Hmm?"

Now, just for the record here I couldn't let Reggie impugn my masculinity...the strength of my will...my total control over my own body. I mean, Reggie is a guy...yeah, he's nice and we have fun, but him, *him make me cum?* I had to laugh. Oh woe is me; laugh was most definitely the wrong word to be punning on here.

"Ha, Reggie you're nuts...why in the world would anyone think that you or any guy could make me cum...against my will at that?" I asked him, not mentioning my past history with guys like Ronald. "Ha, that's laughable."

Sticking out his hand he said, "So, it's a bet then...hmmm?" He was eyeing me, one eyebrow raised.

How could I refuse? I had been challenged...or was it I who had made the challenge? If I didn't take Reggie's challenge I would be saying that "yes", he could make me cum and that I was not the master of my own body. I was backed into the proverbial corner.

"Okay, it's a bet," I said and held out my hand as well. "But what is the bet for?"

"Good!" Reggie exclaimed and we shook hands, him holding my hand much tighter than necessary...making me look down where our hands clasped. "And I can use any means I deem necessary to make you cum? Hmmmmmmmmmm?" he added.

"Well, yes! I guess? But the bet is that YOU make me cum. You can't run in a ringer...like the Asian princess to get me off," I demanded and felt good once more about being assertive.

I was feeling confident that this was going to be an easy bet to win. Poor Reggie would just expend a lot of energy and I would win. Again I asked... "Now, just what all does the winner get?"

Reggie just grinned at me and said, "Well, if I can make you cum then I get to continue to have my way with you for the rest of the weekend... whatever I want to do. But, in the unlikely event that you should be able to resist and not cum, then *you* name it. What do you want?"

I didn't have to think long or hard about that. I was so eager to have my way with the Asian princess, I didn't even think about what I was agreeing to.

"I want to spend the weekend with the Asian princess and she has to be my slave," I babbled. "Whatever I want her to do she will have to comply."

My tongue was hanging out at the thought of Reggie's Asian princess and her being my slave.

"Agreed!" Reggie announced and I found that I had now agreed to this absurd contest.

What had I done? Oh well, but there was no way Reggie would be able to make me cum...and when I win...I'll get this Asian princess to do with as I please...and I will please a lot. I was pleased with myself after all and feeling real smug.

"Okay," Reggie said, snapping me out of my Asian princess daydream. "Be at my place Friday afternoon and I will begin the process of making my favorite sexy author spew his man juices for me...and then I will have you for the entire rest of the weekend. Ha, ha...see you on Friday Timmy."

With that Reggie left with a real skip in his step and I was left feeling weakly confident that I would be the one prevailing on Friday.

So, Friday came in a hurry and I went to Reggie's without changing from work, suit and tie still on. I rang Reggie's bell and waited. The door cracked open and I was surprised to see the Asian princess peeking at me through the crack in the door. Her eyes twinkled and her beautiful red lips broke into a smile.

"Mista Timmy!" she sang and the door opened wider.

Her beautiful bare arm snaked out and her delicate but firm hand with the bright red nails grasped my wrist and she pulled me toward the door.

"Asian Princess!" I stuttered in surprise, calling her by the only name that I knew her as. "What, what are you doing here? I was supposed to meet Reggie. We have a...a bet!"

I was going on in total confusion.

The Asian princess pulled me into the room and closed and locked the door. She was barefoot with bright red nails on her pretty little feet. She was wearing a silk sleeveless robe with Asian print of black and silver, with a black silk sash around her little waist. The robe presented a "V" all the way to the sash and her lovely olive skin and cleavage was visible to my hungry eyes. And I could see flashes of her bare legs and what looked to be a black thong as the robe parted beneath the black sash. Her shiny black hair was pulled back into a ponytail and she had exactly the right amount of makeup on to accent her eyes that glowed at me. My cock literally leapt in my suit pants at the sight of her.

"Hee, hee," she giggled. "Reggie tell me about bet. Hee, hee! But I don't think you gonna win Mista Timmy!"

And with that said she started pulling on my suit coat. She moved behind me and pulled my suit coat off my shoulders and tugged it quickly down my arms.

"Uh Asian Princess...I feel so foolish calling you that, Asian Princess that is," I stammered, nervously tweaking at the knot in my tie. "What uh, what is your name? You see, Reggie has never told me."

I turned around to face her as she folded my suit coat and ceremoniously placed it on a table. She then turned once more to face me, an adoring sort of look in her eyes.

"Tees-U," she giggled. "My name Tees-U! Reggie no tell you my name?"

She looked questioningly at me and she came back to stand very close and her little hands went next to my necktie and pulled, loosening the knot. Oh my word.

"Uh no, Reggie has always referred to you as the Asian Princess... just the Asian Princess," I stammered as she worked at my tie. "You see, he knows how Asian women excite me and so he has always teased me about you and you being his Asian Princess."

I was stammering more and more as I stood there mesmerized by her dark sparkling eyes as she tugged on my tie and grinned as she finally pulled it from my shirt collar. She folded it neatly and placed it with my suit coat.

"Making you comfortable Mista Timmy," she giggled sexily.

"Uh, Reggie told you about the bet? He told you...the whole thing?" I asked, reaching to tug at my tie that was no longer there.

Watching her and thinking about the bet and having this luscious Asian dish for my own was causing my cock to stir in my suit pants...soon to be obviously erect. Make me comfortable? Fuck of fucks, she could do with me as she pleased I foolishly thought.

"Tee hee! Yes Mista Timmy!" Tees-U said as she again returned to me and now began working on the buttons of my dress shirt, making me comfortable indeed. "He tell me ALL about you bet. Hee, hee, an you gonna lose! Hee, hee for you Mista Timmy." As she spoke and giggled she punctuated that statement by pulling on my shirt to get the tails of it out of my suit pants. My word, I was being stripped by the Asian Princess. But I was so aroused by her magnificence that I could not think to ask her to stop.

"Tees-U what are you...what are you doing?" I managed to finally question my little Asian beauty.

I could see flashes of her pert but ample breast when her robe parted. She pulled on the shirt and pulled it over my head...causing me to bend over. Having not unbuttoned the sleeves the shirt pulled inside out as it trailed down my muscular arms.

"Tee hee hee hee hee!" Tees-U giggled as my shirt came off over my head and then she yanked it hard, popping the buttons on the cuffs.

"Mista Timmy, I make you comfortable and prepare you for bet with Mista Reggie! What you think I do?"

She cooed lovingly and folded the wrinkled shirt and placed it with my suit coat and tie. As I heaved breathlessly at the sight of her my cock twitched in my suit pants, my balls churned and my man tits bubbled up hard and erect on my muscular well-toned chest.

"Wait a minute!" I demanded as her sexy little bare feet padded back toward me and her silk robe parted below the sash, showing me her bare legs and flashes of her black thong panties. "Uh, just wait a minute here!"

She smiled seductively at me and her fingers grasped my belt buckle.

"What are you doing?" I asked her again, trying to get my thoughts in order. "I mean... It's Reggie that I have a bet with. But, if you'd like to have a roll in the hay...I'm ready for you." I smiled a stupid gawky grin back at the Asian beauty.

"Hee, hee, ah no, we no roll in hay! Hee, hee!" she giggled. "Hee, hee! I just get you comfortable and ready for Mista Reggie. Reggie be wiff us quickly, no? Then he make you lose bet. Hee, hee!"

And with that she pulled my belt from the loops in my suit slacks and hung it around her neck.

"You're getting me ready for Reggie?" I asked. "Hey, that's not part of the bet. He's cheating. I told him that for him to win he could use you to make me...uh...mmmm..."

"Hee, hee! Cum? Make you cum?" Tees-U asked me as she grabbed for the button on my suit pants. "No, no, Tees-U not make you cum. Hee, hee! That's what Reggie going to do to you. I just get Mista Timmy comfortable and ready for Reggie! Hee, hee!"

She tugged on the clasp at my waist and I almost fell into those dark, deep pools she had for eyes. Then I felt my zipper slide down and felt the pressure of her small but educated hand as it moved with the zipper along my stiffening shaft. Loosened and then released from her hands my pants slid down my shapely muscled legs and fell to the floor, piling up at my ankles.

"Hee, hee! Tees-U no make Mista Timmy cum!" she chortled as she squatted in front of me, bumping my cotton tent with her forehead.

I believe that was on purpose. Then she busied herself with removing my suit pants, causing me to raise one leg at a time and pulling them over my shoes.

"Nice suit!" my Asian tormentor said. "I take off so you don't get cum on it. Hee, hee! Mista Reggie make Mista Timmy cum! Hee hee!"

She kept teasing me about this. She also had gotten me so hot and worked up. So, she was sort of priming the pump...but I guess neither she nor Reggie was breaking our wager rules. Maybe they were stretching the rules...at least I was stretching...in my underpants.

"Tees-U, I don't think this is quite fair," I complained to her as she folded my slacks and placed them with the rest of my clothing, leaving me standing there in my erection tented cotton briefs, dress socks and shoes.

But she was not through with me yet.

"I mean, Reggie and I made a wager...and if I win...uh, if I win...then you...you, the Asian Princess will spend the weekend as my slave!" I said in a husky sounding tone of voice.

I grinned and my cock twitched at the thought of me having the Asian beauty naked and at my disposal. Tees-U returned to me and ran her hands over my stomach and up to my chest and toyed with my erect nipples, causing me to twitch and giggle.

"Mista Timmy very tickly man...no?" Tees-U asked me.

"No, hee, hee, no...don't do that...NO, I'm not ticklish," I said and tried to grab her wrists but she quickly avoided my grasp and then pushed me backward till I fell into a big stuffed chair.

"Mista Timmy, you so ticklish, you easy! Hee, hee," she said as she untied my shoelaces and popped my shoes off my feet. "You wait right there. Tees-U fix you some refreshment before Mista Reggie make you cum! Hee, hee..."

She left me sitting there in my underpants and socks as she poured and mixed something in a glass at a nearby table.

"Well, I may be ticklish, but I plan to find out just how ticklish Tees-U is this weekend," I said, speaking confidently to my Asian dream.

She turned on her bare feet causing her silk robe to flair, giving me a glimpse once more of her black thong covered mound beneath. She grinned big and said, "Oh, you no find out how tickly Tees-U is!" She calmly stated this as she padded back to my near naked form. Then, she leaned over, allowing me to gaze into the top of her gaping silk robe. She luscious pert breasts hung there with dark erect nipples.

"Here, drink this!" she said and pushed the glass to my lips.

I drank deeply from the glass as my eyes drank in Tees-U's upper assets. Emptying the glass I asked, "Why do you say I won't find out how ticklish you are?"

Tees-U grinned up at me as she knelt at my feet and began pulling off my socks...scraping my soles and causing me to flinch and giggle.

"Oh Mista Reggie have special plan for his Mista Timmy," Tees-U said as she got my socks off my feet. "You cum and Tees-U go. Hee, hee, hee, Tees-U make joke. You see Mista Timmy, Mista Reggie gonna make you cum and then Tees-U gonna go and leave you with Mista Reggie for rest of weekend. Hee, hee. Tees-U not be here for Mista Reggie fun with Mista Timmy."

Listening to what she said made me a little nervous. But, I was bound and determined to win this bet and have Tees-U, my little Asian princess as my sexual slave for the weekend. I could withstand the sexual advances and ministrations of another guy. After all, I was straight. Tees-U kept playing with my feet...once they were bare. Not really tickling me... but just teasing my toes and soles, just on the verge of tickling.

My cock remained hard in my underpants and I was beginning to feel flushed...maybe a little lightheaded. And my cock all of a sudden seemed to want to get harder and harder...my balls were shifting in their sac.

"How you feel Mista Timmy?" Tees-U asked as she raised her eyebrows and smiled seductively at me.

"I-I uh, feel a little funny, kind of lightheaded," I stammered. "Say, did you put something in that drink?"

Somehow I knew I had been drugged...

"You look a little reddish, hee, hee," Tees-U giggled, sounding fiendish now. "And you dickie look like it trying to get out you undie pants. Hee, hee, just a minute...I need to finish get you ready for Mista Reggie."

And Tees-U began to move quickly around me connecting straps to my thighs, ankles, around my waist, chest and lo and behold, on my wrists. Then, she began to connect them to pulleys that she pulled down from the ceiling. And me, I was just sitting there watching her strap me up and then she pulled a little remote out of her silk robe pocket. She pressed a button on the remote and the pulleys began rising toward the ceiling taking me and my strapped up limbs with them. As they raised my legs my arms were pulled outwards, spreading me out in a very vulnerable position, oh my word, but I was also forced into a squat or a sitting position if you would...which I would find out later would put my virgin asshole (hardy, har and har) very much into play.

"WH-what's happening...Tees-U, what are you, what are you doing?" I dazedly questioned my Asian beauty and she stood there and watched me splay out in front of her.

Once I was suspended above the chair she stopped the pulleys and then shoved the chair over into a corner...and there I hung.

"I told you, I get you ready for Mista Reggie to make you cum," Tees-U reminded me. "He gonna make you cum big time...and Tees-U gonna have weekend off. But you and Mista Reggie gonna have a fun weekend...or at least Mista Reggie gonna have fun, hee, hee!"

Somehow I was not comforted by her words.

But, she wasn't through with me yet. Tees-U went to the nearby table and brought back a pair of scissors. She proceeded to cut my underpants off me.

"Wait, wait a minute!" I cried in my flustered and excited state. "Now what are you doing? You can't do that! My bet was with Reggie... You can't help him get me off, uh, make me cum..."

"Oh I not help you cum," Tees-U laughed. "Like I say, I just get you ready for Mista Reggie...but, he gonna really make you cum."

And when she finished cutting my underpants she grasped the waistband in front and slowly pulled the rag of material that was between my legs. Thus, my cotton underpants...or what was left of them...dragged across my strangely enflamed and erect cock...and I thought I was going to shoot my load right then.

"Oooooooooh, uuuuuuhhhhh, mmmmmm Teeeeeees-U ooooooooo myyyyyyyyyy" I groaned and my cock twitched and jumped as a result.

"Oops, Tees-U have to be careful," my Asian beauty laughed. "That Viagra you drink really am powerful stuff. Don't you think?"

Her eyes sparkled at me with that female gleam of "I got one over on you" look.

"Now, Tees-U have to go..." she said, sounding sad almost. "Mista Reggie be in to make you cum in just a minute...but since we have hour I know you gonna have fun before you cum...but, you gonna cum for him...I just know you will. So, I may see you next week. Have fun Mista Timmy!"

"Tees-U, wait...don't leave...you can't leave me like this...Tees-U..." my voice trailed off as the sexy Asian princess slipped out of her silk robe... so that she was wearing only a little black thong panty.

She smiled at me, wiggled her breasts at me, draped the robe over one arm, turned and was gone before I could utter another word. I was left dangling naked from the ceiling with my entire body exposed and vulnerable to whatever Reggie or anyone wanted to do to me. And that damned Viagra Tees-U had tricked me into drinking had my cock standing tall and I could tell that I was oh so sensitive to the touch.

The door closed behind her and I was left in my naked suspended anticipation. That sexy little Asian princess Tees-U had really prepared me for Reggie by capturing me, stripping me naked and then getting me suspended and secured in a quite vulnerable position. And to top it off she had fed me a Viagra laced drink and teased me to the point of almost leaking. Shit, and now I hung there with my hard cock pulsing but untouched and the heat from the drug affecting both heads.

I jumped as the door opened and Reggie came charging into the room...his big Asian toothy grin preceding him. I then noticed a naked Tees-U smiling and winking at me as she wiggled her fingers "bye-bye" and closed the door.

"Timmy, my man!" Reggie chortled, taking in the sight of me. "Tees-U has gotten you into a quite a predicament it would appear. And judging by the clock it didn't take her long. So, you must have been very cooperative buddy."

Reggie was simply laughing at me hanging there naked, in a totally excited state and position.

"Reggie, this is not fair, you had Tees-U get me naked and all worked up. That was not part of the bet, plus, she slipped me some Viagra...man, that is not fair," I complained.

"Tsk, tsk and tsk!" Reggie said and grinned at me with his dancing eyes as he took in the sight of my naked trussed up and vulnerable body. "Timmy, our bet was that I could use anything I wanted. I did agree that Tees-U couldn't get you off."

As he spoke Reggie stepped between my spread legs and lifted my dangling balls. He jiggled my gonads a bit with one hand while he used the nails of his other hand and lightly glided them up the underside of my rock hard cock. Chills coursed through me at what felt like hundreds of miles per hour.

"Did the Asian Princess touch you?" Reggie asked, knowing the answer as he fondled my balls in his hand. "Oh man, nice nuts Timmy, real fucking nice...it's going to be my pleasure to drain these puppies for you..."

I could see Reggie's teasing face as I felt his palm jiggle my ball sac some more...feeling the growing weight of my testicles in his hand and all while his other hand teased my erect cock directly.

"Ah, ah! OH aaaaaaaAAAAAAaaa!" I moaned...and grinned big and then Reggie quickly withdrew his hands.

"Timmy buddy, you are leaking already man, and hardy har, har for you I've hardly even begun the process of draining those balls of yours," Reggie chuckled meanly. "Now, I asked you a question. Did the Asian Princess touch your cock? Hmmm?"

The guy was trying to piss me off with that smug, I got you under my thumb look. But, you know, the reality of it was, he did have me under his thumb, so to speak that is.

Looking down at my red and dripping cock I was already beginning to be nervous about this bet that I'd made. I mean, I had bet Reggie that HE couldn't make me cum. And I was confident of that...at least I used to be confident of that. But then, I had let his sexy little Asian Princess strip me, truss me up and suspend me from the ceiling, and before all that she had clouded my mind by tricking me into taking a large dose of Viagra. Woe is me and my word, I never need Viagra to rise to the occasion, but now with a Viagra swirling in my innards I would be erect to the point of insanity buds. So, at this point I was developing a great deal of lack of confidence in my sexual defenses. Then, I replied to Reggie's question through trembling lips, "Ah, no Reggie, no, she didn't actually touch my cock. But man, she didn't have to...she, she's, she is so sexy, so DAMNED sexy...and she was barefoot...and, and she had on that barely closed silk robe...and man, I could tell she was naked, naked except for some little black thong panties. You know how she turns me on...and you know how I love ladies little bare feet...and you had her dressed so danged provocatively...barefoot and all. Reggie, that's cheating...and, and then to top it all off, she topped me off by slipping me a Viagra laced drink...that is totally not fair man...not fair at all." I was in trouble almost from the beginning of this whole stupid bet and I think that Reggie knew my weaknesses and had already exploited most of them. He simply grinned and grinned.

"Timmy my sexy author you..." Reggie laughed fiendishly and stepped to one of my raised and bare feet, grasping it around the center. "My Asian Princess just set the stage for me, you of course being the star on that stage that is. You said yourself that she did not touch your cock. So I did not violate our agreement at all. I said I could make you cum...and I will Timmy, *I will.* In fact, from the looks of your cock right about now you're pretty close to losing our bet and spending the rest of the weekend at my pleasure. Ha, ha for you buddy boy. You are gonna cum and cum... actually I think you will cum your brains out. So after you've done just that I hope that you will have a good excuse for your upcoming absence this weekend...for your lovely wife that is."

Reggie just grinned at me, squeezed my raised foot and I looked at him in utter disbelief...utter disbelief that I had let myself get into this danged predicament. Then, Reggie winked at me and said, "You know what Timmy?" In response I dumbly nodded my head "no." Reggie continued by saying, "I know you will try your best to mentally block me from getting you off. So, I thought I would crumble your mental defenses before we even get started." And with that, Reggie moved his hand up my foot that he was holding and grabbed the toes of it, my left foot to be exact and pulled them back, stretching my wrinkled soles. From the moment he had grasped my bare and raised foot my heart pounded with fear and awful anticipation. Then, Reggie used one finger on his other hand and ran it from my heel, to my arch to the ball of my foot. OH MY WORD!

The sensation was quick and struck me like electricity. My leg jerked in response and I tried to pull my foot away. Reggie's finger retraced its path but this time going down from my toes to my heel. My leg jerked again and again, but I could not escape and the sensation was too much for me not to respond.

"EEEEEEE, oooooooooo, Reeeeeeeeegiiiieee, hee, hee, hee, hee... d-don't eeeeee, don't do that bud..." I squeaked.

"Timmy, Timmy, Timmy, you are one ticklish guy," Reggie said meanly as he discovered my worst weakness. "You are not going to be able to think of one thing except the tickling that I'm going to bring to you... and that cock of yours is going to get harder and harder until I decide to bring you off. WOOO WOOO!" And meanly, Reggie added more fingers to my stretched and tickled left foot.

"Reeeeeeeeeheeeegeeeeee! STOOOOPPP!" I started...then gritted my teeth and flexed.

I was determined to overcome this...I was not going to let Reggie subdue me with tickling. God knows enough people have in the past, hardy, har and har for me. I groaned out, "Reggie...I, I am not ticklish...that does not bother me...at, at all." The truth be known, he was already driving me nuts. I was just barely able to keep from breaking into loud peals and gales of laughter. But, I sensed that I was weakening and that Reggie would go beyond my breaking point.

"Timmy," Reggie scolded me. "You are so silly. I know for a fact that you are one of the most ticklish guys in the world. See? Watch what happens when I use these horse hair paint brushes on your ticklish soles, koochie, koochie koooo Timmy..."

"FUCKING fucks, you came prepared didn't you Reggie?" I moaned as he produced the horse hair paint brushes from his pants pocket.

With that, a new more intense tickling sensation shot up from my bare feet. I believed that I could feel every single stiff prickly bristle in each of those danged brushes...one on my left sole and one on my right as the guy mock-fully painted the bottoms of my bare feet. The bristles danced at my heels and twirled up across my flexing, bared soles. When they reached my toes they poked and prodded the pads of each of my piggies and then individually invaded the sensitive spaces between my toes. There were hundreds and hundreds of little prickly bristles and each one seemed to know its job was to tickle my poor feet.

At the brushes first touch my eyes shot wide open...actually they almost bugged out...my mouth flew open...but nothing but spittle came out. My breath left my lungs faster than my vocal cords could collapse on the wind. So, the sound was no more than a quick violent wheeze. But, then my natural reflexes took over... I gulped in air and that's when the real laughter started.

"AAAAAAAHAHAHAHAHHAA EEEEEE HEEEEEE HHEEEE HEE HEE WOOOOOOOO HOO HOOOO HOOO" I roared.

I must have been comical to look at and listen to, because Reggie was grinning from ear to ear.

Now, while my brain was occupied with the intense tickling that had just started on my bare feet my already stiff and leaking cock bounced in sexual excitement. It was already red with exhilaration and had started leaking. But now, clear, sticky pre-cum almost flowed from my piss slit. You see, besides being extremely ticklish, tickling is a major sexual turn-on for me. As much as I dread being tickled there's a secret part of me that loves it, and hates it, and loves it, oh woe is me and my word. The Viagra and the Asian Princess' teasing had brought me to a Pre-Reggie sexual edge... but now the tickling was sending teasing sexual shockwaves up and down my leaking cock. My body jerked and pulled in the suspended straps. But gravity virtually kept me in one place even though I pulled back on my legs, trying desperately to get away from the tickling brushes...my whole body would move toward my feet, in affect leaving my feet right where I didn't want them to be...being brush tickled by Reggie.

"OOOOOOOO hoo, hoo, hoo, hoo, hoo, hoo! EEEEEEEEE, hee, hee, hee, hee, hee! BWAAAAAAAAAA, haa, haa, haa, haa, haa, haa, haaa!" I laughed and laughed and well you get the picture.

I was a chorus of the most comical laughing noises you'd ever want to hear. My feet are very, very ticklish...but they are not my most ticklish area. And even though I couldn't put together any coherent thoughts at the moment I was praying that Reggie would begin and end his tickling of my feet. Hell, this was bad enough.

I finally felt my laughter subsiding. I was able to breathe deeply. I had too... I felt like I had been running sprints. Then, I noticed that Reggie was just standing there observing my big, red wet cock...it still pulsing and still leaking. I thanked God for small miracles as Reggie had stopped tickling my bare feet.

"Timmy, your cock is going to spew before long, and you're going to lose the bet!" Reggie chided me with confidence.

I was getting very nervous now. The tickling was total torture. But at the same time, it is a major sexual turn-on for me. And Reggie was using all that to his advantage and to what looked like what would be my eventual demise.

"Look here Timmy; see what I have for you?" Reggie asked and held up some elastic straps with Velcro fasteners on them.

And between the two sets of straps was a single strap with a nest of feathers on it.

"Timmy my man, guess what it is!" Reggie said as he beamed.

I shook my head and just looked. I knew that it couldn't be anything that I would enjoy or that would benefit me, not in the position I was in. I continued to shake my head.

"It's a little invention of mine," Reggie informed. "You see, it straps onto your thighs like this..."

And he proceeded to attach the straps around the very tops of my thighs. He made some adjustments and then stepped back to show me that my cock and balls were now smothered in the nest of feathers strung up between my thighs. OH MY WORD! The feeling was not exactly tickling, but it was definitely stimulating...all those little feathers rubbing around, up and down, just all over my cock and balls. I could tell in a flash that this would keep me hard.

Then Reggie jostled my suspended body and the nest of feathers just wiggled and wiggled all over my manhood and jewels. The feeling was almost too much...but then at the same time it was not enough!

"You see Timmy; these feathers will be very, very stimulating to your big prick and your weighty balls...very, very stimulating indeed. They will tease you till you think you will want to cum your brains out...but guess what my man?" he asked, as if I knew.

I just shook my head again and moaned at the sensations already coming from my loins from the gentle movement of the feather nest.

"I didn't think you would appreciate my little invention, hee, hee!" Reggie teased me. "As I go about tickling other parts of your nakedness and you wiggle and dance in your bonded position the feather nest will also wiggle and dance. And since your cock and balls are nested snug in the feather nest they will be teased and teased and teased. But, you will be teased only to a state of your frustration...because these feathers will not give you enough friction to allow you to cum. Oh trust me my trussed up buddy, you will want to cum. In fact Timmy, you will beg me to get you off, thus losing the bet. How about that?" Reggie looked hungrily at me as I began to take in what he was saying.

"OHHHHHH, AAAHHHHH! Reggie, now don't do this...this is totally not fair man!" I gurgled. "AAAAAHHH! That danged thing is teasing my cock...Oh man Reggie...that thing is teasing my balls...OH, oh, oh...my balls are beginning to ache...Please stop this..."

Dang it all, I was already beginning to beg Reggie. But the guy had other plans. Reggie's wiggling, scrabbling fingers dipped into my hairy exposed armpits and he exclaimed, "Here we go Timmy, and off you go to Laugh City my man, kichey, kichey, kooooo buddy!"

"AAAAAAAAAAAA, ha, ha, ha, ha, ha, ha, ha, ha, ha!" I went off into a rattle of screaming laughter.

I laughed and laughed and jerked and wiggled in vain attempts to get away from those tormenting fingers. And my wiggling was causing the nest of feathers at my crotch to play all over my cock and balls...teasing and tickling the sensitive and enraged flesh...but it only teased, as Reggie said it would do, it only teased. It did not offer any sign of taking me over the orgasmic edge. And we all know that that was Reggie's plan.

"AAAAAAAAAAAAA, hee, hee, hee, hee, hee, hee!" I continued to guffaw and laugh and wiggle and be teased by the feather nest at my crotch. "Reeeeeeegie, hee, hee, hee, hee, hee, hee! STOOOOPPPP oh, ho, ho, ho, ho, ho, hee, hee, hee, hee, hee! OOOOOO, hoo, hoo, hoo, hoo, hoo! Y-you're drivin' meeeeeeee hee, hee, hee, craaaaaazy. EEEEEEEEE hee, hee, hee, hee, hee, hee!"

And my cock was just pumping and pumping out clear, sticky pre cum...but I was not getting any closer to shooting my load of loads.

Reggie did stop... I thought he was showing me mercy. But, actually, he just wanted me to settle down so he could taunt me some more.

"Timmy my man, are you ready for me to make you cum...and win our little bet?" he asked me. "Hmmm? Are you ready to call your wife and offer some excuse as to why she won't be seeing her handsome hubby this coming weekend? Hmmm my man?"

He grinned at me, knowing that I was in sexual agony, but also that I was competitive and I was bound (literally actually) and utterly determined that I would not, WOULD NOT become his weekend sexual toy...tickle toy...or whatever he had planned to do with me. I could not let him succeed here. I had to hold out. Reggie knew this and this just made the little game that much more fun for him.

"No!" I muttered. "I'm not going to cum...I don't care whaaaaaaaaat..."

Reggie cut off my tirade by jiggling my suspended body, causing that feather nest to wiggle over my cock and balls.

I-I don't care whaaaaaaaaat you, you, you do...I'm noooooooot going to leeeeeet you make me cuuuum!" I bantered, trying to sound convincing both to Reggie and mostly to myself.

I had to convince myself that I would not let him get me off. I mean how could I stand an entire weekend of this kind of teasing...no way man.

"Nice resolve Timmy my man!" Reggie said as he grinned at me and then stepped over to a table and returned with two nipple clamps. "Maybe these little devices will help convince you that you need to cum for me."

"Reggie no! NO! Don't put those...OUCH!" I prattled.

But my complaining didn't stop Reggie as he placed a nipple clamp on each of my stiff, sensitive nipples, what I call my man tits...the teeth of the clamps bighting into my tender flesh.

"OUCH! OUCH!" I bellowed and wiggled in the restraints, making the feather nest torment my cock and balls all the more.

It hurt like hell initially, but then slowly the pain subsided or the area was numbed somewhat by the squeezing clamps, maybe both, but they served as yet another distraction to my ability of trying to keep my mind on preventing Reggie's success...which was to make me cum...and he was making it hard...and believe me I was HARD.

Now with my cock and balls being ever caressed by that damned nest of feathers and now my nipples being bitten by Reggie's infernal clamps the guy was free to attack yet another area of my naked suspended and very vulnerable body.

Yes, I was giggling and moaning as the nest of feathers teased and tickled my male equipment in my crotch. No matter how hard I tried I just couldn't be still, what with the tickling at my crotch and the nipple clamps bighting my man tits...and woe is me, when my body moved the nest of feathers goggled and tickled and teased my balls and cock and whatever else they managed to wiggle against my crotch. I was in a no win situation. Oh I was being teased to no end...but at my crotch it was a very light and very tickly sensation...not nearly enough to make me cum.

Then Reggie walked around behind me.

"Timmy lets see how ticklish you are in your pits again huh?" he asked and with that he grabbed me underneath my arms and this time really dug and wiggled his fingers in my hairy sensitive armpits.

"WHOOOOOOOO HOOOOOOO HOOOOOO! EEEEEE HEEEEEEE hee, hee, hee!" I ranted loudly and I was off on another breathless laugh track as Reggie played my armpits like they were his piano.

"Whoo weeee Timmy, you are one ticklish boy. I don't think I've ever seen anyone as tickly as you buddy, hee, hee," Reggie said with a smirk as he enjoyed himself.

After a while I could not hear a word he said. I was too busy laughing my ass off. Oh yes, my cock and balls were being treated to an extra heavy dose of feather teasing now from the nest of feathers as my body jerked and twisted from Reggie's armpit tickling. When I wasn't laughing and trying to inhale I was moaning at the sexual teasing my cock and balls were getting. My poor cock was leaking heavily now. What with the Viagra I had been tricked into swallowing and all the teasing that had been done and was still being done to me I did not wonder why I was so stacked up in the cock. GAWD, I could see the thick green veins in my cock, they were so pronounced and pulsing. FUCK all but I needed to cum so badly it was like my life depended on it. But if I did cum Reggie would win the bet. I was in no position to think or enjoy...or in this case be concerned with my very obvious sexual excitement. My balls were tightening up...but the feathers didn't offer enough friction to push me over the orgasmic edge. Instead they just fanned my sexual flames and added fuel to my sexual fire...but alas, would not let me explode.

I did not want to cum...I did not want to give in to Reggie. Because that would mean that I had lost our bet. That would mean that Reggie had taken control over my body. It would mean that he had been able to coax an orgasm out of me against my will. I was a straight dude...but Reggie was making me wish he would take hold of my cock and bring me home.

Reggie stopped tickling me...and let me come down from my breathless guffaws. But, he kept jostling my body so the nest of feathers would do their work. Now, I was no longer laughing...but I was moaning at the sensations coming from my crotch.

"Timmy?" Reggie called out to me, sounding somehow far away.

"Oh....aaahhh...mmmmm...ahhhh...what? WHAT?" I moaned.

"Are you ready to cum for me? Are you ready to shoot your load and lose your bet?" Reggie teased me and made sure to wiggle my suspended body.

"Oh maaan, ahhhhhh ooooooo oh man, aaaahhhhh mmmmm! Cuuummm, oh noooo Reggie...no aaaaahhhh mean aaaahhhhh ooooooo Oh Reggie stooooo p oh, oh man mmmm!" was my garbled response.

"I think you're ready to lose this bet young man..." Reggie stated sternly. "I don't think it will take much for me to claim my prize, you being my prize Timmy."

And with that...Reggie oiled up his right hand with some lubricant he had brought just for the occasion...pulled the nest of feathers away from my cock and balls and grasped my meat like it was a huge pickle. I gasped loudly and arched my head back and the guy started stroking and stroking and stroking. My balls tightened and tightened some more and my cock was straining under the friction. I bellowed and moaned from deep inside myself. Reggie gave my cock a number of rapid brisk strokes...then my entire body arched and he used his thumb and tweaked the furculum right beneath the mushroom shaped head of my cock... Oh my word, that was it. I yelled and every muscle in my body went taut... My balls almost drew up into my body and I shot hot gooey ropes of thick white cum from my piss slit. And Reggie, bless his heart...Reggie aimed my love stick right at my head as I slowly brought it forward again...so that my face was soon dripping in my own cum. For a moment I jerked and flinched as Reggie squeezed the last droplets of my milky goo from my cock. Dang, I was beaten, defeated, sexually topped by another guy...I had lost my bet...and now I would realize my fate.

Reggie laughed at me as I hung limp and sweating from my suspended position. I was now a dishrag. I had been tickled, teased and forced into orgasm...and not just an orgasm but one of those off the Richter scale, earth shattering orgasms. I had experienced the kind of gusher that makes a guy's teeth itch.

"Well Timmy...you lose! Or should I say...I win! Ah, ha, ha for you my handsome bud. Now then, since this is Friday night...you lose the entire rest of the weekend!" Reggie reported with confident glee as he took the tit clamps off my nipples.

"RRRRRRRRR..." I seethed as the blood rushed back through my tenderized man tits at what felt like hundreds of miles per hour.

I just looked up at him through my cum filled eyes...exhausted and beaten.

"But Timmy, you are such a good sport, letting my Asian Princess capture you and tie you up like this; I'm going to honor you with your request," Reggie said as I looked at him in confusion. "You know you wanted the Asian Princess for the weekend...right?"

He was taunting me; I could see the taunting in his eyes.

"Y-yes..." I replied weakly.

"Well, you and the Asian Princess will be together the entire weekend!" Reggie said and grinned fiendishly as he announced this wonderful news to me.

"Really? Really?" I began to say and perked up from my exhaustion at this news.

"Yes...but with one slight adjustment," Reggie replied and grinned expectantly at me. "I'm going to call the Asian Princess back and I'm going to give YOU to HER for the entire weekend. So, you two will be together...just not exactly as you had planned. In fact...*you* my man will be *her* prisoner, her tickle toy, her sexual plaything...you will do whatever she wishes. Won't that be great?"

Reggie was just beside himself with his announcement. He loved that he had won the bet and could do with me as he pleased. I slumped back into my suspended bonds...JEEZ! I had wanted the Asian Princess for the entire weekend...and now Reggie was giving her to me...OR, should I say...giving ME to her...for the entire weekend.

As I thought about what I would tell my wife when I called her to let her know that I would be away for the weekend (perhaps a last minute business trip I had to attend) I wondered if I would be able to survive...

Timmy Backman meets Christopher Trevor and Vince (maybe)

"OHHHHHHH! OHHH YEAH, oh my word, oh my!" Timmy Backman bellowed in blindfolded darkness as he shot his load of Southern spunk, unswervingly and directly down Christopher Trevor's throat as he sweated and gyrated on the tabletop.

Timmy Backman, tickle hero, tickle star and constant unwitting tickle victim lay atop a cushioned massage table, stretched out on his ripped and muscular back, clad in nothing more than his trademark white kangaroo pouch boxer briefs and Christopher Trevor's trademark black nylon ribbed dress socks. For this special occasion however Christopher Trevor had opted for his tickle star to wear black sheer thick and thin calf length ribbed silk socks, what are also sometimes referred to as tuxedo socks or a guy's wedding socks. (The style of thick and thin silk socks is usually that the toe and heel sections are solid black nylon while the center of them are thinly sheer, sometimes ribbed, ribbed being all the more sexier.) The author claimed they were much more festive looking for the event...the event being that upon the release of the book "Timmy's Ticklish Trials", the author, Christopher Trevor himself, the CO-author and star, Timmy Backman in the flesh (and in the black socks of course) and Tickle Master Vince, a guy who if anyone *did* brought Ronald Greene (Timmy Backman's tickle captor and tormentor) from the book to life, should all meet, in person, finally. And meet they would in a hotel room in New York City to celebrate the release of this fateful tome that had brought three very much likeminded guys together. But Timmy had to wonder when Vince would be arriving, seeing as he and Christopher had been in the room for some time now that morning to afternoon since he had checked into the hotel... and the author had been killing time milking his star repeatedly...every half hour to forty five minutes to be exact. Not that Timmy was complaining, it felt great to be treated this way, even if he had to be tied up and blindfolded for it...even if Christopher tormented him a bit by putting tit clamps on his fleshy nipples for fifteen minute intervals, just to get Timmy real stacked up in the department of his manhood. But he also wanted very much to meet Vince in the flesh. After all he and the handsome muscular black guy had had many stimulating and ticklish IM conversations over time on the internet...HARDY har and har Timmy thought as Chris took the blindfold off him again. The way Vince had tormented him erotically on line made the tied up, tied down Timmy wonder just what the handsome African American master tickler would heap on him in person...*when* he arrived that is... Timmy recalled the tickle promises that Vince had made where he was concerned. Timmy's cock churned in his kangaroo pouch underpants as he thought of Vince's promise to kidnap him away from his family for some tickle time torments. He recalled Vince's dark proposition to tickle him crazy and then tickle him some more, once he had the handsome Southern laddy in his clutches that is. Timmy remembered the internet games that Vince had made him play, the consequences being that if Timmy won he would not be tickled...but if he lost, well, he didn't need three guesses to know how quickly he would be tied up and tickled, hardy har and har again the handsome Southern guy thought. Even while miles away from Vince when they would chat on their computers Timmy felt a certain submissiveness where this man was concerned. If Vince told Timmy not to touch his cock while he teased him in IM fashion Timmy found himself obeying perfunctorily. Being tied up there wasn't much poor Timmy would be able to do to stop the muscular African American guy from doing to him...tickle wise that is...and inwardly the handsome Southern gentleman had to wonder if he really would want to stop Vince. Oh decisions, decisions, Timmy had to chuckle to himself.

Vince, also known to submissive and ticklish Timmy as "Tickle Master Vince..." The tickle master who had, on numerous occasions challenged the ticklish laddy to numerous computer games...just to be inside Timmy's head and to see how the ticklish boy would react under pressure...

Christopher had met the handsome African American tickle master in person and had seen him at his tickling best with another buddy. The author knew that Vince would come to the hotel with all his equipment, his bag of bondage tricks as he called it. If poor Timmy thought he was tied up now he would not believe the positions and bondage he would suffer/enjoy when Vince arrived. But for the moment the author had his handsome tickle star all to himself, and he planned to simply feast on and enjoy him...he had waited long enough for this after all...

"Wow, how many times does that make now?" Timmy asked his captor as he lay with his shoulders hunched up off the table, watching as the author made his way to the end of the table, directly to his tied up black socked feet.

"I've lost count," Christopher said as he leaned down over one of Timmy's black socked and tied feet and slurped and licked at his solid silk covered toes.

Timmy wiggled his toes in ecstasy and chills engulfed him as his author buddy played suck and slurp with his feet...the part of his body that he seemed to treasure the most. Christopher held Timmy's foot by the sole with two hands as his head bobbed up and down as he serviced it. He also pressed his thumbs in a massage-like fashion into the balls of Timmy's black socked tootsies, sending definite feelings of ecstasy through his very special buddy. Timmy knew that Christopher Trevor adored his feet...the author also adored his big cock, seeing as he had once more left the beefy root dangling temptingly and invitingly out of the fly opening of Timmy's white kangaroo pouch style boxer briefs... And being that as it was the tied up handsome Southern gentleman knew it would not be long before Christopher was once more sucking him off...either that or Vince would arrive and the laughter would begin...his own Timmy thought woefully and hopefully at the same time... Timmy was never able to decide just how much he really hated/loved/loved/hated/hated/hated/loved/loved being tied up and tickled. His cock hung slightly erect, very slimy looking and stained with saliva and cum from his boxer briefs and Timmy, now with his eyes uncovered glanced over at the end table where the small pill bottle that contained the Viagra tablets and the pitcher of water and water glass were set. As his feet were serviced most lovingly Timmy laid his head back on the table and sighed contentedly.

"Dang it all, Viagra," he said to himself and chuckled. "Looks like this guy plans to make a meal or two out of my spunk..."

Christopher's mouth opened wider and he engulfed all five of Timmy's socked toes into his mouth. He sucked heartily and Timmy swooned atop the table, his tied up hands balled into fists behind his back. Chills traveled up the laddy's spine, up his calves and legs, into his thighs and into his pulsing and over-used cock. Christopher dribbled oodles of saliva onto Timmy's socked toes and sucked it up heartily, sending hyper-chills through the tied up guy. His muscular back arched and he crooned "Oh my word..." in his Southern sounding accent. Once more Timmy's root began to harden to full mast. He smiled thinly and wondered when Chris would clamp his man sized tits again...

"Oh my, oh my fucks," Timmy groaned.

The feeling in his spent cock was astronomical and he could not believe that he wanted/needed to cum yet again.

While he had been packing for his trip to New York City Timmy Backman somehow figured he would wind up in the weave of some tightly knotted ropes and a blindfold...not to mention on the ticklish end of a feather or some other infernal ticklish equipment that he was sure Vince would bring to torment him with. Timmy could not deny the churning in his cock and balls as he thought of his buddy Christopher and him finally meeting. He knew that the author would find some way to get him into a bondage and black sock situation. He smiled through pursed lips as he packed extra black socks in his luggage as he thought this. And sure enough, now, his hands *were* securely roped behind him at the wrists in a criss-cross type of fashion, allowing the guy a tad of movement back there as he writhed and squirmed atop the table. His black socked feet were roped tight with mounds of white rope adorning his ankles, his muscular and sexy legs spread wide and his ankles tied off to the legs under the table. Timmy the ticklish laddy, as he was sometimes called found himself in a most vulnerable and sexy position...while in the clutches of his author buddy... He was a straight guy, a straight guy who loved and adored his beautiful wife, but there was no denying the effect that his author buddy,

Christopher Trevor could have on him. Timmy knew in his heart that the author was crazy about him and being that as it was, he knew that Christopher would drink from him till his balls were drained...and then some.

When he was done packing Timmy slammed his luggage shut, just as his sexy wife Stephanie came into their bedroom. He breathed a quick sigh of relief. He was sure she would have questioned him on all the new pairs of black socks he had packed along with his other belongings. Most of the black socks were gifts for Christopher, but he knew also that he would more than likely be made to wear a pair of them or two...it was the author's most intense fetish after all. Throughout the tickle novel they had written, "Timmy's Ticklish Trials" Christopher had had Timmy's feet clothed in black socks more often than not. Granted Timmy did get his inner wish to be bare foot tickled at intervals in the story, but eventually the guy always wound up with his black office socks back on his big sexy feet. The sight of her handsome husband dressed in a suit and tie and wingtip shoes always sent the beautiful Stephanie over the edge. Ever since her girlfriend Valerie had introduced her to the finer, more erotic sexual practices she loved the thought of her executive husband stripped to his socks and briefs and at her mercy... It was amazing to her what a submissive nature her handsome and muscular husband had when it came to their sex lives. It also drove her wild how her husband always plumped up nice and big in his underpants for her whenever she decided to play her kinky games. The "Spinning Chinaman" device down in their living room had taken the poor Timmy on many a spinning journey while he was clad in just his socks and underpants, sometimes just his socks so that Stephanie could have some mean cock teasing fun with her darling hubby...and Stephanie planned to subject her hubby to still more...as soon as he returned from this impromptu business trip that he had to go on in New York City. It had come up all of a sudden and Timmy explained that there was just no getting out of it for him... Stephanie sidled up behind her husband in his Brooks Brothers navy blue suit and encircled her arms around him, pulling him close to her, pressing his shapely buttocks that she adored against the part of her that he adored. She swooned as she thought of the night before and how he had made the letters of the alphabet in her pussy as he ate her relentlessly...and right after that, *and right after* she had cum numerous times he told her about the business trip he had to attend to in the heart of the big apple.

As she held tight to him he turned around in her embrace and smiled the smile that always melted her heart...and hardened her tits...and made her pussy moist...

"So you're sure you're only going to be gone three days?" she asked him, straightening his tie for him as he held her tight.

"From what I know, yes," he replied, his hardness pressing against her through his suit trousers. "Like I told you Stephanie, *I have to go*...it really is a ticklish business thing that I have to take care of..."

She giggled like a schoolgirl, knowing how her handsome hubby hated yet loved being tickle tortured...

"Funny how you always use that word when it comes to these annoying little things that can crop up in one's life, ticklish that is," Stephanie cooed and tugged at Timmy's tie.

Now, as he lay tied atop a massage table in a hotel room in the heart of Times Square, Timmy recalled the way Stephanie had looked at him when he was done packing. He wondered what she would think now if she saw her handsome spouse and what kind of predicament he was currently in...

Blindfolded again Timmy sipped water from the glass to wash down yet another Viagra tablet that Christopher Trevor had placed on his tongue...after he had serviced Timmy's black socked feet for more than the usual fifteen minutes that time...

"OHHHHRRRR SHIT," Timmy bantered in the once more blindfolded darkness as he felt the tit clamps snapped onto the very tips of his hyper-sensitive man sized nipples. "Dang but that smarts Christopher..."

"Sure as hell Timmy my laddy," Christopher teased his CO-author and constant tickle victim, giving his dangling root a squeeze as it again hardened and reddened between his splayed legs. "But it also gets your core here nice and stiff. Admit it Timmy, you have real sensitive nipples for a guy..."

"Oh yeah, oh my, I do at that, I have real sensitive nipples for a guy," Timmy repeated nearly verbatim, the sound of his Southern accent driving his captor crazy with lust.

Being blindfolded Timmy could not see how Christopher Trevor was salivating just at the thought of once more drinking from the tied up guy's font. The author held Timmy's cock with one hand and then reached into the guy's kangaroo style boxer briefs and ceremoniously brought out his very plump kiwi-sized testicles. The tied down guy gasped breathlessly as his testicles were handled. Timmy's balls were all sweaty and musty scented. When he felt Christopher's tongue begin polishing them he swooned and tears of ecstasy soaked his blindfold...

He was enjoying himself so much...but he knew that all this sucking of his cock, the scoffing down that Christopher was doing with his seed, the servicing of his black socked feet and now the polishing of his balls would come to an end...and he would be tickle tortured. And he also knew that because he had shot his load a few times already how he would be ultra-ticklish when the time came. For whatever the fuck the reason Timmy always became more tickle sensitive after he had shot a load or two...or three...

"OHHHHH, or four..." he whispered as his author buddy once more slurped him into his mouth and started sucking. "OHHHHH my word..."

Timmy's clamped nipples tingled as Christopher Trevor worked him once more by the root...

"Ohhhhhh dang, what a way to go, what a way to be done," Timmy swooned and licked his lips.

When Timmy Backman had arrived at the airport in Atlanta Georgia he did not expect any tribulations or untoward occurrences to happen that might delay him or cause him to miss his flight. As usual the very organized, very structured executive had planned this trip like any other business trip...except that this was a tickle book related business trip, something that his buds at the bank he worked at just would not be able to relate to...but then again, one never knew Timmy surmised gleefully. As he climbed out of the cab he paid the driver and an airport bellman quickly tended to Timmy's one piece of luggage. He tipped the cab driver and the airport bellman, thanked them and as his luggage was moved onto the conveyer belt to be brought to the plane that would carry him to New York City our unwitting tickle hero entered the airport...

Looking at his watch Timmy saw that he still had an hour and a half before his flight took off. Since all the new security measures had been put into place at airports Timmy, like most other travelers knew that it was best to be at the airport at least an hour and a half to two hours before takeoff time. He sauntered through the airport with a slight bounce in his step, his cock at half mast in his kangaroo pouch style under shorts that he was wearing under his suit pants. Timmy purchased a paperback book and a box of mints at an airport newsstand and figured at that point he would go through the security check and sit and relax in the plane's waiting area for his flight to be announced. Holding his paperback book and slipping his box of mints into his suit jacket pocket he approached the security checkpoint. He was the third in a short line of a couple of other business suited guys. Like the other two men before him Tim reached down to unlace and slip his wingtips off his feet. It had become standard airport procedure since September 11th, 2001.

"Damn, I hate taking my shoes off in public," the burly suited guy ahead of Timmy said as he turned and looked at Christopher Trevor's buddy.

"Yeah, I know what you mean," Timmy agreed, standing up straight, his shoes held in one hand and his paperback book in the other.

"Its always just my luck that I have an embarrassing hole in one of my socks or that my feet are all sweaty and everyone gets a whiff of it as I check through the scan point," the guy said to Timmy. "My name's Ronald by the way..."

A chill went up Timmy's spine as he said, "Nice to meet you Ronald, I'm Tim, Tim Backman," recalling another person he knew by the name of Ronald. He wondered if this was some kind of ominous omen where this trip was concerned. Ronald was the villain after all in the book he was headed to New York to celebrate the release of...the villain who had so brazenly kidnapped him in the story...

"Everything okay there Tim?" Ronald asked Timmy. "You look like you've just seen a ghost or something."

"Uh, yeah, sure, everything is great," Timmy replied and wiggled his toes in his navy blue nylon dress socks.

As he glanced down at Ronald's brown socked feet he said, "Well, no holes in your socks this time" and smiled at the football player shaped guy.

"Nope, and no stink either," Ronald chuckled.

"NEXT!" came the sound of a demanding female voice, startling the two men out of their reverie.

"Whoops, looks like that's me Timmy buddy," Ronald said and dashed through the metal detector.

As Ronald was checked through and scanned by two very sexy, very curvy looking female security guards Timmy found himself sweating nervously. Ronald? A guy named Ronald? I've met a guy named Ronald at the airport Timmy asked himself incredulously. He tucked his paperback under his arm and loosened his tie a bit, wiggling his toes under his socks at the same time, his cock throbbing in his suit pants.

"NEXT!" the blond curvy female security guard bellowed.

"Oh yes, oh, that uh, that would be me," Timmy gasped and walked through the metal detector after placing his book and shoes in the plastic basin provided by the airport.

The walk-through metal detector beeped slightly and the two women gestured for Timmy to approach them. Ronald was getting his shoes back on as the two female guards scanned Timmy with their rectangular shaped metal detectors. The first one, a tall curvy blond girl fitted into her security uniform like a glove, her short skirt, stockings and low heeled shoes driving the laddy into a frenzy. The second female guard was a redhead with beautiful green eyes and a body like a dancer. She too filled out her uniform most sexily. As he was instructed to do Timmy stood with his arms held out in a wing-span fashion as they trailed their scanning wands over him. It tickled slightly when they scanned his ribs and stomach areas and he squirmed on his thin socked feet. When the blonds' scanning wand trailed over his suit jacket pocket it made a loud beeping sound.

"Oh my, that's my fault," Timmy said in his Southern accent, sounding real sexy and macho at the same time. "I totally forgot to take my house and car keys out of my pocket."

As he reached down the redhead said to keep his arms where they were and that they would tend to his keys. Timmy did as he was told and the redhead reached with well manicured fingernails into his suit jacket pocket, extracting his keys. She dropped them in the plastic bucket along with Timmy's shoes and his paperback book and then resumed scanning him along with her blond partner. Timmy noticed that two other security guards, both of them males had taken over scanning the passengers who had been in line behind him, to keep the crowd moving along he supposed.

While he was in the clutches of the two beautiful women Timmy watched as other passengers were checked through with no problem, retrieved their shoes and other belongings and went along their way. His shoes however remained right where they were. Looking around he saw that Ronald was long-gone as well. As the two female security guards again ran their scanning wands over him Timmy squirmed a bit as they once more not on purpose tickled his ribs and stomach areas.

"No beeps that time ladies," Timmy said with a warm smile. "Guess I'm good to go huh?"

"No Sir, I think being that you caused the detectors to go off like that we should do a thorough search," the redhead, the more stern of the two guards said, holding her wand against Timmy's buttocks as she spoke.

"Uh, I'm sorry Miss, a more thorough search?" Timmy asked, slowly lowering his arms.

"Yes, it's all very routine you understand," she said, sounding reasonable yet strict at the same time. "How long till your flight?"

Timmy glanced at his watch and said "An hour and twenty minutes."

"Plenty of time for a thorough search," the blond security guard said and in a sweeping motion yanked Timmy's watch off his wrist and dropped it into the plastic bucket with his other personal effects.

She scanned his now naked wrist...

Then, a few moments later, carrying his shoes, his watch, his keys and his paperback book in the plastic bucket Timmy walked into a private security room with the two female security guards...

"I must say ladies, that was a bit humiliating for me, being brought here amid all the stares from people in the airport," Timmy said, sounding irritated as he set the plastic bucket down on a small table in the gray painted bare walled room.

The redheaded security guard explained that it was procedure when someone set off the metal detectors and that if he wanted he could complain to the airports upper management when they were done with him.

"Now Sir, your name please," the redhead said, picking up a clipboard and pen from the table.

"Tim Backman," Timmy replied, still sounding a bit irritated that this had befallen him, but unable to deny that the two sexy ladies in their security guard skirts and uniforms were making him tent up in his suit pants.

The redhead wrote his name on a blank sheet of paper along with the other information that Timmy recited for her, namely the nature of his trip, how often he flew, where his destination was, etc. As he spoke the blond security guard sidled up next to him and as softly as possible asked him to remove his suit jacket. Timmy complied and she hung his suit jacket on the back of a chair. The redhead put down the clipboard and asked Timmy to once again stand with his arms out in a wing-span position. He did as he was told and the two women trailed their scanning wands over his upper torso. But as they scanned his armpits area and his stomach and ribs he bent over slightly and squirmed, giggling a bit.

"H-hey, hee, hee, hee, easy with those wands ladies, I'm a tad ticklish here," Timmy said, sounding totally gullible.

The two security lovely's looked at each other across Timmy, rolled their eyes in their heads as if to say, "The things we have to put up with" and then the blond asked Timmy to please remove his shirt and tie and his under shirt, if he was wearing one.

"What?" Timmy asked as he lowered his arms, him sounding like he was in a state of disbelief now. "What is this, some kind of strip and tickle search?"

"Sir, Mr. Backman, I assure you, we are not here to tickle you, but yes, it is a sort of strip search," the redhead said and as Timmy reluctantly undid the knot in his tie he watched her pick up his suit jacket from the chair where it hung and she ran her scanning wand over it a few times.

No beeps or buzzes emanated from her wand as she scanned his suit jacket. He noticed how as he unbuttoned his crisp white dress shirt how the blond security guard was staring a bit transfixed-like at him.

"So uh ladies, you two know my name, what all are yours?" Timmy asked, practically blushing now as he handed the blond security guard his shirt and tie.

He stood before the two women now with his muscular bare chest on display, his big man-sized nipples totally erect. They both seemed to take in the sexy way his chest hair trailed down his ribcage and to his stomach region in a straight line.

"I'm Bonnie," the blond replied as she pointed at Timmy's belt.

"And my partner here is Jane."

"Hmm, Bonnie and Jane, nice to uh, meet both of you," Timmy prattled on, his hands trembling as he reached to undo his belt.

Bonnie handed Jane Timmy's shirt and tie and like she had done with his suit jacket she scanned the shirt. No beeps or buzzes emanated...

"Say ladies, is this uh, is this really necessary?" Timmy asked as he undid his belt buckle.

"Very necessary Mr. Backman," Jane said, her wand held in her hand as if she were wielding a paddle. "You set off the metal detectors out at security check. What we're doing here is standard procedure. If you would prefer to have two male security guards conduct your strip search that can be arranged." As she reached for her cell phone Timmy quickly bantered, "No, no, this is fine..." and shucked his suit pants down around his ankles. He stepped out of his pants and handed them to Jane. She held his pants up and when she ran the wand over the back pocket of them the device buzzed loudly.

"And what do we have here Mr. Backman?" Jane asked him as she reached into the back pocket of his suit pants while he stood there now clad in just his white boxer briefs and blue dress socks.

"It uh, it's probably just my wallet," Timmy said nervously. "More than likely my credit cards with the magnetic strips on them are setting off your wand."

Jane extracted Timmy's wallet from his suit pants pocket and looked at him as if he were totally guilty, but of what he was not sure. His cock was by now throbbing in the pouch of his boxer briefs in a mixture of trepidation and arousal as these two sexy women worked him over verbally.

"Why didn't you place your wallet in the plastic bucket at the security checkpoint Mr. Backman?" Jane asked him and dropped the wallet now in the bucket.

"It uh, it slipped my mind Jane, I mean, Miss, it slipped my mind Miss," Timmy bantered nervously. "Oh my word..."

"Please stand with your arms spread out while we do a body hair search," Bonnie said, rubbing her wand over Timmy's lower back as she spoke.

Timmy did as he was told and he knew that once he was standing in a wing-span position again his erection in his underpants would be beyond evident. The two women stood at his sides and when they trailed their wands over his hairy and bushy armpits he exploded into gales of loud laughter.

"WHOOOO, hee, hee, hee, hee, hee, hee, hee!" Timmy laughed loudly and instinctually lowered his arms and used his hands to block his ticklish pits. "Oh please, come on now, do you really think I have something tucked in my armpit hair?"

"Mr. Backman, do you find all this to be funny?" Jane asked him, holding up her wand. "Because we're trying to do this as quickly as possible so you can be on your way and we can get back to our posts in the airport."

"No, no Jane, I mean, no Miss, I do not think this is funny, not in the least..." Timmy squawked.

"Bonnie, please use the wire cuff to restrain Mr. Backman's hands behind him so that when we search his other areas he will remain positioned properly?" Jane suggested.

"R-restrain my hands?" Timmy bantered as the blond beauty produced a pair of plastic wire handcuffs from her utility belt. "Is, is that really necessary?"

"Hands behind you please Mr. Backman," Bonnie said and as Timmy did as he was told he saw Jane pulling on a pair of latex tight fitting gloves.

"Oh no, oh my word," Timmy whispered and his asshole seemed to contract.

The two women looked at each other almost fiendishly as Bonnie tied Timmy's hands tightly in the wire cuffs...

"OHHHHHHH..." Timmy moaned a few minutes later as Jane squatted behind him, pulled his underpants down in back and inserted a latex glove covered finger into his rosebud of an asshole. "ULLLPPP"

As Jane probed and dug in his hole Timmy stood facing Bonnie with his hands restrained behind his back. Bonnie had cleavage to die for and then some. As his hole was searched by the uncompromising redheaded Jane he could not take his eyes off Bonnie's chest, her nipples poking seductively against her uniform blouse.

"This is uh, rightly embarrassing I would have to say Miss," Timmy said to Bonnie as he arched his back and nearly hauled himself to his socked tiptoes, his biceps bulging as he tried to maintain his balance. "I mean, having my hole searched in such a fashion, you see what I mean..."

"It will uh, it will be over soon, we still have to search your socks," Bonnie said and with a grin on her face and unseen by Jane she kissed one of Timmy's nipples, giggling like a real blond as she did so.

Timmy's head spun and he wiggled his toes as Bonnie kissed his nipple again and Jane probed deeper in his hole... His cock churned in his underpants... Search his socks? He wondered what the fucking fucks that was going to be like...

It wasn't long before Timmy found out exactly what Bonnie had meant about searching his socks and what it would be like and how he would laugh himself into a thither because of it...as the laddy found himself after his anal probe half on and half off the table in the private room. The plastic bucket with his personal belongings in it had been set aside on the floor and it was now Timmy atop the table on his lower back with his socked feet dangling off the side, his legs swinging back and forth. His hands, still restrained behind his back he had balled into a big fist and he laughed like crazy as the two female security guards were hunkered down at his dangling socked feet and were running the tips of their scanning wands back and forth against the bottoms of them. Bonnie and Jane each held Timmy by a calf to keep his feet steady as they scanned and scanned the bottoms of his feet.

"WHOOOOO, HAHAHAHAHAHAHAHAHAHA!" Timmy cackled crazily, sweating atop the table as the two bitch security guards seemed to be getting their jollies as they made him suffer.

"I ask you again Mr. Backman; do you find all this funny somehow? You think this is all a big joke?" Jane asked him as she held tight to his socked calf and trailed her scanning wand over and over the bottom of his foot.

"I-I don't think its funny at all, poor me laying here with my danged under shorts pulled down in back and just my office socks," Timmy cried. "HAHAHAHAHAHAHAHAHA! But with the way you two are a tickling the daylights out of my danged feet I can't help but laugh and laugh... HAHAHAHAHAHAHAHAHAHAHAHA!"

"Why do we get all the crazy passengers?" Jane asked Bonnie.

"L-ladies, I- I assure you, there is nothing in my danged socks,"

Timmy panted through his peals of loud laughter. "I am not trying to smuggle anything into New York City that way..."

"You would be surprised Mr. Backman the things that some people will do..." he heard Bonnie say as she and Jane did their dirty work.

"HOO, HOO, HOO, HOO, HOO, HOO, HOO, HOO, HOO!" Timmy laughed, sounding like a hyena as he did so...

"Okay, I think he's clean," he heard Jane say a short while later. "Let's let him get dressed so we can get back to our post."

"Th-thank you Jane, I mean, thank you Miss..." Timmy said, catching his breath as the two guards stood up, took him by an upper arm each and helped him off the table.

"Take the restraints off him and meet me back out at the post," Jane said to Bonnie as she exited the room, closing the door behind her.

"Well, I can see who's in charge," Timmy said with a boyish grin as Bonnie stood in front of him.

"She's just very job oriented," Bonnie said and looked at Timmy adoringly. "Sorry about the embarrassing tickling Mr. Backman..."

"It uh, its okay Miss, just uh, please free my hands so I can climb back into my suit and be on my way, I don't want to miss my plane after all," Timmy said.

Bonnie looked at him for a moment more, kissed him on the lips once and then stood behind him to undo the wire restraints.

"Why'd uh, why did you kiss me first Bonnie?" Timmy asked as he massaged his wrists once they had been freed.

"I didn't think you would let me afterwards," Bonnie responded and walked out of the room.

Timmy chuckled, gave his erection a squeeze through his underpants, hiked his underpants back up over his ass, pulled his socks up and quickly got dressed...

"OHHHHHHH..." Timmy hemmed loudly yet again as his author buddy Christopher Trevor once more scoffed down his pearly white thick juices. "Oh my Lord never came so much in such short a period of time I must say..."

Timmy writhed and squirmed real sexily atop the massage table as Christopher drank him down yet again. The tit-clamps on his nipples started to drive the poor guy crazy, really making his man-sized tits feel real sensitive as he spurted his most recent load down his buddies' throat.

"Amazing, totally amazing what that Viagra stuff can do for a guy huh Christopher?" Timmy panted behind his blindfold.

"Sure as hell," Christopher replied a few seconds later after he let Timmy's soft cock slip from between his lips, giving the tip of it a few kisses as he did so. "God almighty, but your cum tastes so good Timmy."

As Timmy's once again spent manhood flopped to the side Christopher quickly took the clamps off his good buddies' nipples.

"OOOOOOOOOO…" Timmy swooned, his blindfolded head arched back as the feeling of the blood rushing back into his nubs sent chills through his muscular being.

"Yeah, I know bud, it feels real twisted when the clamps come off huh?" Christopher asked.

"You can sure say that Christopher," Timmy responded and if he hadn't been tethered to the table at the socked ankles he would have flown off it for sure when Christopher leaned down and slurped one of his jutted up nipples into his mouth. "OHHHHHH, oh my word of words…sucking my danged nipples now huh?"

"Got to do something to kill time till Vince gets here buddy…" Christopher said and quickly resumed suctioning Timmy's sensitive feeling nipple with his tongue, lips and teeth and gently squeezed and tweaked the other one with his fingers.

"Yeah, uh, speaking of that, when in tarnation is that guy going to get here?" Timmy asked Christopher as the guy sucked his nipple harder and harder. "I don't think you'll be getting any more milk from me buddy… least of all from my danged nipples…OH but my word that does feel good though…"

Timmy smiled behind his blindfold as he felt his buddies' hands roaming up the sides of his stomach area as he lay atop the table while his nipple was sucked and the other one was tweaked and squeezed…

After Timmy had gotten back into his suit, knotted his tie and tied his shoes he quickly dashed to the waiting area for his flight. As luck would have it he still had ten minutes before his flight departed and he saw that his fellow passengers were now boarding. He cursed the two female security guards for making him almost miss his flight…and he cursed Bonnie especially for not giving him the relief he was obviously craving in his under shorts when she had kissed him. Ah well the laddy figured, he was going to be meeting with Christopher Trevor and Vince the tickle master. He had no doubt that he would be getting more than his share of relief in his most private of areas, hardy har and har and thank you very much buds...

When Tim boarded the plane and headed for his window seat he was surprised to see his new friend, the guy he called "The new Ronald" sitting in the aisle seat next to his window seat.

"Well hello there Tim Backman," Ronald said jovially as he quickly stood up to let Timmy enter the seat and sit down.

"Well now, this sure is a surprise Ronald," Timmy chuckled, straightened his tie and got himself comfortable.

"Say, what happened with those two security guards back there Tim?" Ronald said as he too settled into his seat again.

"Trust me when I tell you man, *you do not* want to know," Timmy replied and saw that his seatmate was holding a trade sized paperback book on his lap.

"Hmm, that looks familiar," Timmy said, looking at the back cover of the book.

"It should, and it's the craziest thing," Ronald said and held up the book "Timmy's Ticklish Trials" by Christopher Trevor. "I feel like I've been plucked from the pages of a book Tim. The lead character's name in this book is your name, Tim Backman. And the guy who captures and tickle tortures him is named..."

"...Ronald..." Timmy said gripping the armrests of his seat as a look of disbelief came over his handsome face.

"Something wrong buddy?" the new Ronald asked Timmy as he stared straight ahead.

"Well, yes and no Ronald, somehow I think the omens are all making sense now," Timmy replied as he thought of Bonnie and Jane tickling his socked feet. "What uh, what's your last name? Its not Greene is it?"

Ronald chuckled and held up the book...

"You have read this haven't you?" the new Ronald asked Timmy as the laddy continued to stare straight ahead with a look of horror on his handsome mug.

"You might say that Ronald, you just might say that," Timmy said softly.

"My last name isn't Greene, it's Rosalie..." the new Ronald said and Timmy's Adam's apple was suddenly very prominent above his necktie knot as he swallowed hard.

So uh, Ronald, what are you all heading to New York City for?" Timmy asked his new friend, desperate to change the subject.

"I live there actually Tim, I own a bookstore in the village and I just recently acquired the Christopher Trevor books," Ronald said. "I was in Atlanta visiting a buddy of mine who owns a bookstore there. He said the Christopher Trevor books were selling pretty well so I decided to get them for my store too. What uh, what are you heading to New York for Tim?"

"I'm going to meet Christopher Trevor in person for the first time," Timmy said and he and the new Ronald looked at each other in disbelief.

Timmy was recalling that fateful meeting on the plane and his mind was jolted back to the present for the moment now while Christopher Trevor spoke on his cell phone as he cradled it against his ear on his shoulder. As the author spoke on his cell phone he was also tying Timmy's upper body to the table he was spread out on. No more being able to lift his upper body while being sucked off the handsome Timmy Backman thought as he was tethered tightly even more-so now.

"Yeah, okay that sounds great," Christopher said into the cell phone, Timmy watching with his blindfold now made into a makeshift gag, one of his own navy blue dress socks that he had worn with his suit for the trip crammed into his mouth with the blindfold now tied over it, keeping his musty tasting sock jammed in place.

Timmy was only able to lift his head off the table now as Christopher was obviously speaking to tickle Master Vince.

"Well, I'm glad you finally made it into Manhattan but what made you think it would be easy to find parking?" Christopher asked his tickle buddy.

Christopher smiled and listened as Vince was obviously telling him just how bad the traffic in Manhattan was.

"No, we'll wait for you here, its no problem," Christopher said and looked into Timmy Backman's beautiful eyes as the guy watched himself being tied down at the upper torso. "You and I can go out to dinner later.

We'll leave Timmy here while we're gone, tied up of course, ha, ha! He won't mind. We'll bring him back something to eat though. Timmy and I have been having some wonderful quality time together, haven't we Timmy? Here, say hello to your tickle master Vince."

Smiling mockingly Christopher put the cell phone to his tied down buddies' ear. Timmy heard Vince's deep voice saying "Hi Timmy, how's my ticklish buddy doing?" All Timmy could do in response was utter a feeble sounding "Mmmfff..."

"Yeah, I know just what you mean buddy," Vince replied and cackled meanly. "But keep your socks on, I'll be there soon enough and trust me you'll be doing a lot more than making muffled gagged guy sounds..."

"MMMFFFF..." Timmy responded again, chewing on his dress sock and the taste of it roiling down his throat, making his head spin.

He also could not believe what he had heard Christopher say, that he and Vince would leave him tied up in the hotel room later on while they went out for dinner.

"Ah yes my handsome Southern laddy, I can picture you right now," Vince cackled meanly in Timmy's ear. "I would be willing to bet a month's salary that my good buddy Christopher has you tied up real tight and I'll bet another month's salary he's got you wearing just those black socks he loves so much and maybe...just maybe your trademark kangaroo pouch style under shorts. HA!"

"MMMFFFF..." Timmy ranted into the cell phone as his cock dangling from his boxer briefs churned.

"Yeah, I bet I would win that bet huh my ticklish Timmy?" Vince laughed again as he drove. "My ticklish Timmy B..."

Timmy nodded a few times instead of making muffled sounds into the phone, realizing that he could not possibly communicate with a sock/gag crammed in his mouth. Christopher took the phone from Timmy's ear and placed it back against his...

Christopher said good-bye to Vince for the moment, hung up the cell phone and looked down at the tied up Timmy Backman, admiring his bondage handiwork.

"That was Vince," Christopher said and Timmy simply nodded in understanding. "He's here in Manhattan but he's having a difficult time finding parking...said it'll be another half hour or so at the very least before he gets here."

Timmy nodded again, aggravated that his buddy had gagged him with one of his own used socks. What a shitty thing that was to do to a poor guy Timmy thought. But then, he didn't have much choice in the matter, seeing that in a way he had handed himself over to Christopher for this trip...and to Vince as well it seemed... The two guys were going to make his weekend full of tickle madness, of that he had no doubt at all...

"So, it looks like we'll have to kill some more time before Vince gets here," Christopher said, looking quizzically at his handsome bound tickle star. "Got any suggestions on what we could do buddy?"

Timmy rolled his eyes in his head in disbelief, swallowed more of his own funky sock taste and wiggled his toes under his sheer thick and thins...

"I got it, how about another Viagra?" Christopher asked and whipped the gag off Timmy's mouth, followed by yanking the balled up navy blue sock from his captive's craw.

"Yeah, just what the doctor ordered huh bud?" Timmy asked, licking his lips to moisten them as his cock churned and Christopher a few seconds later fed him another Viagra tablet. Timmy gulped it down with a goodly amount of water as his buddy held his head up from behind. As Timmy drank down the Viagra Christopher pecked him lightly on the cheek and whispered "Thank you Timmy..."

While the Viagra took effect Christopher blindfolded his tickle buddy again and spent a few minutes sucking the laddy's socked toes...

While chills and thrills enveloped him Timmy's mind wandered in the throes of ecstasy...

"You're going to meet Christopher Trevor, the author of this very book, in person when you get to New York City?" the new Ronald asked his very perplexed and amazed plane-mate.

Timmy had to wonder what the chances were of his being tickle tortured by two gorgeous female security guards at an airport. But it had happened, it had happened bud. He also had to wonder what the chances were of meeting a guy named Ronald in line with him at the security checkpoint at that same airport...and what were the chances that that guy named Ronald would be reading the latest tickle book by his buddy Christopher Trevor? All this was too scary of coincidences Timmy thought as he pulled his tie down a notch as he sat next to the guy named Ronald Rosalie on the plane that was about to take off for New York City. (Ronald Rosalie?)

"Yeah, that's who I'm going to be meeting, yes indeed Ronald," Timmy replied.

"Jeez, so you're telling me here that you're Timmy Backman from the story?" Ronald asked aghast. "Do you mean to tell me that I'm sitting here with a fictional character made flesh?"

"Interesting way of putting it, but I suppose you could look at it that way Ronald," Timmy replied and ran his hand down his tie.

Then, the two men sat silently and enjoyed the feeling of liftoff as the plane barreled down the runway and was then airborne...

"Say, I have an idea Timmy," Ronald said, his eyes suddenly lighting up. "How about you come to my store in New York while you're there?"

"That sounds great, but somehow I think most of my time is going to be spent with my author buddy," Timmy said with a grin. "Somehow I get the feeling that I'm going to be real busy and tied up with all this book business..."

The two suited men laughed and Ronald handed Timmy a business card with his name, phone number and the address of his bookstore in New York City.

"Well, perhaps before you have to head back to Atlanta you could stop by for just a peek," Ronald said, sounding hopeful. "I have an awesome display set up for your buddy's books. Tell Christopher to stop by as well..."

He handed Timmy a second card...

"Hmm, now you really have my curiosity peaked Ronald," Timmy laughed as he took the second card from his new friend. "I think I will try to stop by your store at that before I head on back home..."

"Sounds like a plan to me...Laddy..." Ronald chuckled and a chill crept up Timmy's spine.

The two men settled back in their seats and read their books as the plane headed for New York City...

As Timmy recalled that meeting on the plane he now laid tightly tied down and blindfolded yet again as his author buddy feasted heartily on his newly induced Viagra erection...

"UHHHHHHHH..." Timmy grunted breathlessly, wondering when in hell Vince would finally be arriving, when the tickling tortures would begin and he wondered what the "Christopher Trevor" display of books at Ronald Rosalie's bookstore would look like...

That was one place Timmy intended to see while he was in New York City...but for the moment he could not see much as he felt his balls cooking up yet another batch of Southern Spunk for his buddy Christopher to chow down on...

"Oh my word..." Timmy panted and wiggled his toes under his sheer thick and thins.

After deplaning and collecting their luggage from the carousel Timmy Backman and Ronald Rosalie shook hands, said they would meet again and went their separate ways in cabs departing from the airport...

Timmy arrived promptly at the "Grand Diamond" hotel in the heart of Times Square at eight o'clock that Friday morning. He thanked his lucky stars that in the mornings the traffic in Manhattan was not as intense as it would be when Vince was arriving later on. Christopher had checked into the hotel the day before so his buddy was waiting for him in what would be their room for the weekend. Timmy tipped the cab driver, picked up his luggage and sauntered into the hotel lobby...

At the front desk he found out that Christopher was in room 1018 on the tenth floor...

As Timmy rode the elevator up to the tenth floor the handsome Southern gentleman had no idea what he would be in for. He did know that more than likely Christopher would have everything set up long before he had gotten there, bondage and tickle-wise that is, hardy har and har. At the sound of knocking Christopher dashed to the hotel room door and opened it. He took in the sight of Timmy Backman, his tickle hero, muse and constant story tickle victim standing there in the flesh, *finally*, in the flesh. Timmy, as Christopher was doing took in the sight of his CO-author and tickle buddy. Christopher was casually dressed in blue jeans, a pullover Polo shirt and slip on loafers. Christopher breathed in hard at the sight of Timmy; he was handsomer than his pictures did justice. And to really fit the scene he had shown up clad in a navy blue suit complete with a crisp white shirt, necktie and highly shined black lace-up wingtip shoes. "Well now, and hello Mr. Author," Timmy said as he entered the hotel room, taking in the luxurious surroundings as he stepped in.

"And, I must say, this is very nice," Timmy went on as he put his luggage down on the floor and turned to face Christopher.

Timmy's salt and pepper colored hair and green eyes mesmerized the author. The two men held their arms wide open to each other and hugged tightly.

"At last we meet," Timmy said, sounding so sexy, so Southern, so Senator John Edwards to Christopher's ears.

"Yeah, my fictional character in the flesh," Christopher replied as he squeezed the back of Timmy's neck, his lips grazing the Southern guy's earlobe as he spoke. "My Mister Timmy Backman...my ticklish laddy..."

Christopher's eyes were filled with tears of joy but instead of crying he laughed a bit and then held his CO-author by the upper arms at arm's length. The author really drank in the sight of his star of so many tickle stories, and most especially the novel that started it all, "Timmy's Ticklish Trials."

"Is that what you're going to call me while we're here?" Timmy asked Christopher. "Your ticklish laddy?"

"Hmm, maybe I'll just call you Timmy Backman, my VERY ticklish laddy," Christopher replied and the two men burst out laughing together that time.

Timmy's laugh was booming and sexy sounding at the same time. It sent a true wave of lustful ecstasy through Christopher. As Timmy laughed he pulled the author again against himself and said, "It's really great to meet you Christopher Trevor..." Timmy's strong and muscular arms felt awesomely powerful to Christopher. The author could feel Timmy's bowling ball sized biceps against his back. Timmy was six feet one inch tall and he towered over Christopher's five feet nine inch frame. The author reached up and again ran a hand over the back of Timmy's neck, upwards then against the back of his salt and pepper colored hair.

"That hair that you're tousling and stroking used to be brown with blonde highlights," Timmy whispered in Christopher's ear, sounding unbelievably sexy and Southern once again as he spoke.

"It looks great," Christopher panted as he smoothed Timmy's hair, again fighting his tears that threatened to spill over from his eyes.

Christopher then boldly pressed his lips against Timmy's cheek and kissed him, something the author had been dreaming of doing since they had begun writing and since their on-line friendship had blossomed. Timmy didn't seem to mind so the author kissed his cheek again...

"You're my laddy after all Timmy," Christopher whispered in his special buddies' ear.

Timmy smiled and turned four different shades of red. Never before had he felt so special to someone, so valued. Actually Timmy had been the model for numerous erotic tickle stories that Christopher had written over time. It was something he had never given a thought to throughout his lifetime. More than just a model he was also considered a very sexy and erotic consultant on those tickle tales. As far as Christopher Trevor was concerned no one was better when it came to the tickle tales than Timmy Backman himself.

"Did you have breakfast?" Christopher asked. "I could have something sent up for you if you're hungry."

"Nah, I had something on the plane," Timmy replied. "I'm fine, but thanks still the same... Nice room you got for us...it's uh, really spacious..."

As Timmy looked around some more it was at that moment that he noticed the long sturdy looking massage table that was set up across the room, right next to the king sized hotel room bed.

"...yeah...really spacious..." Timmy said, taking in the sight of the table, slowly approaching it, noting also that a pile of white cotton rope was placed at the foot of the table. "Oh my word...so uh, is this to be my perch Christopher?"

Christopher laughed and took Timmy's upper arm in hand as his "laddy" seemed to be drinking in the sight of the table. Visions of the two lovely female security guards back at the airport flitted through Timmy's mind and his cock churned in his suit pants.

"I had the hotel send up the table," Christopher explained, holding Timmy's arm tight as he spoke. "The white cotton rope I purchased at "The Pleasure Chest" down in the Village area, along with some other things that I'm sure you'll find to be most entertaining. I learned years ago that when one is tied with white cotton rope it doesn't leave rope burns...no telltale signs of a person's bondage adventures..."

"I'm sure..." Timmy said and nervously tugged on his tie.

"After I checked in yesterday I went shopping in Manhattan," Christopher said and let go of Timmy's arm. "I figured if I won at the wager you and I will participate in very shortly I could use the things I purchased on you..."

"And if you lose buddy?" Timmy chuckled, him almost sounding as sadistic as Ronald in the tickle novel. "Remember, I may not be as unlucky in wagers as Timmy in the story was."

"Hmm, well, I suppose that if I lose the wager then the tables will have been totally turned here," Christopher said, mulling it over almost miserably as he spoke. "If I lose you and Vince, when he gets here will get to tickle torture the fuck out of me..."

Timmy laughed and said, "What a switch that would be huh? Christopher Trevor tickle tortured instead of poor ol' Timmy Backman."

Timmy shucked off his suit jacket, hung it in the closet and loosened his tie...

"So, speaking of Vince, when will that fiendish tickle master be arriving?" Timmy asked.

"Some time today for sure," Christopher replied and tugged on Timmy's loosened tie, noting how sexy the laddy looked with the top button of his shirt undone and his tie loosened a bit. "He has some business to take care of and then he'll be here...so for the time being you and I have this hotel room to ourselves. We can uh, do our tickle wager and then have some fun until Vince arrives..."

"Fun...I have to wonder what kind of fun you have in mind for me if I lose that wager Mr. Christopher Trevor Author," Timmy said with a slight giggle.

"Let's just say your blindfold is ready Laddy," Christopher said and again tugged Timmy's tie.

Timmy's cock churned again and his balls felt like they were pulsing and Christopher prayed that he himself would win the wager...the present he had bought for Timmy at Bloomingdales was enough alone to make the author say this prayer. But if he lost he would enjoy the handsome Southern guy in the other direction...so be it...

"So what sort of wager do you have in mind?" Timmy asked with a grin etched on his handsome face.

"Over here please and I'll show you," Christopher replied, leading

Timmy into a smaller room of the luxury hotel room, a room off to the side.

In the extra space of the hotel room Timmy saw two laptop computers set up on a table, two chairs facing the computers. On the computer screens were the graphics for the game "Electronic Hangman."

"So it's to be a word game then?" Timmy asked as he and Chris stepped over to the two laptop setups.

"Sure is," Christopher said. "First guy to lose three games is the tickle victim."

"Hmm, that sounds pretty fair," Timmy chuckled, his hands crammed in his suit trouser pockets as he rocked back and forth on his wingtip heels.

A few seconds later Christopher and Timmy were seated in front of the laptops and playing the game of "Hangman..."

"UHHHHHHHH! OHHHHHHH yes, oh my fucking word of words," Timmy panted in bonded and blindfolded darkness as his buddy Christopher drank yet another helping of thick white juice from his cock font. "That Viagra truly is the stuff of dreams...and nightmares, seeing as I'm the poor guy all tied up and being milked like this..."

Christopher had just the tip of Timmy's cock currently in his mouth. He teasingly swirled his tongue over the very sensitized tip of it, poked his tongue tip into Timmy's piss slit and scoffed down the last remnants of his laddy's latest offering.

"And you thought these balls of yours wouldn't be able to cook up another batch of soup for me Timmy," Christopher said with a grin once Timmy's cock was out of his mouth.

As Timmy heaved for breath under the binding ropes and his face contorted in ecstasy behind his blindfold Christopher could not resist once more moving to the laddy's sheer thick and thin black socked feet and playing suck and lick with them.

"I-I suppose that Viagra really does the trick then huh?" Timmy asked.

"And you as well Timmy, you as well," Christopher breathed as he held onto Timmy's feet by the arches and gently kissed his socked toes. "Vince should be here any minute now Laddy, so I think milking time is over for you...for the moment. I'm sure that I've pumped enough loads from you to make sure that every part of you is hyper ticklish at this point."

"Oh woe is me..." Timmy bantered behind his blindfold and it was then that Christopher trailed the tip of a finger upwards against the bottom of one of Timmy's sheer socked feet.

"WHEEEEEE, oh no, are we starting without Vince?" Timmy squealed...

After the two men had been playing "Electronic Hangman" for a good half hour Christopher had lost at just one of the word sessions while Timmy had lost at two.

"One more to go for you my ticklish laddy," Christopher chuckled as Timmy and he guessed letters for their perspective words of the moment.

"Don't get those ropes ready for me just yet buddy boy," Timmy said, his Southern accent pouring out real thick now, him obviously very nervous at that moment.

He guessed a letter and it was incorrect. An arm appeared on his hanged man on the computer screen.

"You only have one arm and two more legs to go Timmy," Christopher laughed as the letter he had chosen appeared in his current word.

Timmy looked at Christopher miserably as his opponent deliberately chose a wrong letter. An arm appeared on Christopher's hanged man.

"Just biding my time till you lose that session Timmy my ticklish laddy," Christopher said.

Timmy wiggled his toes in his wingtips and sweated as he moved his mouse toward yet another incorrect letter.

"Dang it all, what is that word?" Timmy seethed through clenched teeth, the feelings in his feet awful with tickle trepidation.

His cock churned and he felt glee filled as the next letter he chose was a correct one...

But then, a few moments later it was over...Timmy had lost three word sessions in the game of "Electronic Hangman." The handsome Southern guy slumped back in his chair and looked over at his fiendish buddy, his feet sweating in his shoes.

"Don't get too comfortable in that chair Timmy," Christopher said, reaching over and tugging on his tickle victim's tie. "I'm sure you'll be a lot more comfy stretched out on the massage table and wearing the gift I bought for you..."

"Says you..." Timmy said softly as he and the author got to their feet.

Back in the main part of the hotel room Timmy slowly undid his necktie and unbuttoned his crisp white dress shirt while Christopher took a gift wrapped box from his backpack.

"And what might this be?" Timmy asked as he stood bare-chested in front of his author buddy and took the box from him.

"I had them custom made for you by a tailor at Bloomingdales," Christopher explained as Timmy opened the box and then held up the pair of sheer thick and thin black silk socks.

"Oh my word, direct from our story "Timmy and The Hong Kong Tailor", Timmy said softly and his cock pounded in his suit pants.

"I trust you're wearing your kangaroo pouch style under shorts my laddy?" Christopher asked his buddy mockingly.

A short while later Timmy was stripped of the lower portion of his suit and lying atop the massage table on his back. He had changed from his navy blue nylon dress socks that he had worn with his suit to the ones that Christopher had given him as a gift. He lay looking totally sexy and vulnerable wearing just the socks and his trademark kangaroo pouch style under shorts with his hands tied off behind him while his author buddy slowly and methodically tied his ankles to the table legs. Christopher worked diligently and lovingly as he tied his buddies' feet...

As Christopher tied Timmy's sheer socked feet Timmy looked around the room from his bondage point now. He noticed the small pill bottle and the pitcher of water and the water glass.

"What uh, what's all that?" Timmy asked, gesturing with his head.

"You'll find out when the time comes, and you do too..." Christopher laughed, leaned down and kissed the bottom of one of his tickle captive's socked feet.

"Hmm, so what are we going to do until Vince gets here then?" Timmy asked and that was when Christopher, without a word, blindfolded his tickle buddy, helped himself to the succulent treat that the ticklish laddy kept stored in his boxer briefs and began what would be an all morning till afternoon suck and Viagra fest...

"OHHHHH...OHHHHHH my, oh my word..." Timmy panted at the ecstasy and squirmed under the binding ropes...

"So what do you think Timmy, is this a good way to kill time till Vince gets here?" Christopher asked and quickly slurped his buddies' huge cock back into his craw.

"OHHHHHHH...you won't get an argument from me on that Christopher," Timmy gasped as he was re-sucked into the author's mouth.

After Timmy had cum two times and Christopher ate both helpings the author gave the ticklish guy the first of what would be various Viagra tablets...just to keep his buddy on the ticklish edge for when Vince arrived...

Christopher was actually glad that Vince had delayed in arriving for their Timmy Backman tickle fest... It gave him time to feed off the laddy for a while and utterly drive him batty. Christopher knew that after Timmy shot his load his tickle barometer went upwards. By the afternoon Timmy had lost count of how many times he had spermed so Christopher was well aware of just how very ticklish his laddy was at that moment...

As Christopher drank in the sight of his bonded buddy they heard a knock on the door.

Vince arrives...

At the sound of the knock at the hotel room door Christopher quickly took the blindfold off his tied down buddy.

"So it would seem that Vince has arrived...MMMFFFFF..." Timmy squawked miserably as Christopher again filled his mouth with one of his navy blue nylon dress socks. "RRRMMMMMMFFF..."

As Timmy once more chowed down on his own musty foot scent Christopher walked to the door of the hotel room and opened it. Standing in the doorway Timmy saw one of the handsomest African American gentlemen he had ever laid eyes on. So that was Tickle Master Vince Timmy thought as his head spun and his cock churned. That was the man who had so tormented him internet-wise for over a year at that point Timmy was thinking as he drank in the sight of Vince. Timmy made mewling sounds of desperation behind his sock gag and squirmed under the tight binding ropes. From the look in the African American guy's eyes

A Boner Book

he was most definitely the fiendish tickler he made himself out to be... and then some Timmy thought as he struggled fruitlessly. The tied down Southern gentleman knew just at the sight of Vince that he would soon be laughing his head off crazily. He struggled harder to get loose...to no avail. Christopher quickly ushered Vince into the room and closed and locked the door, not wanting any passerby in the hallway to see that they had a guy clad in just his underpants and socks tied to a massage table in the room.

"Well, well, finally welcome," Christopher said as he and Vince embraced tightly.

Watching from his tied up position atop the table Timmy saw that Vince was six feet tall or better. Even though the handsome black guy was wearing a jacket it was obvious that he was well toned and very muscular. All those jokes he had made about "carrying" his ticklish Timmy away from his family for some tickle fun was obviously possible. Judging from the width and girth of Vince's broad shoulders he would have no problem whatsoever in picking Timmy up and carrying him off...just as Ronald had done in the soon to be classic tickle novel. Timmy could see also though that Christopher did not have tears in his eyes as he hugged Vince. For some reason he was glad for that as a pang of jealousy coursed through his tied up being...

"MMMFFFF..." Timmy bantered as he watched Christopher and Vince hug each other tightly.

Vince had rolled a large-sized luggage on wheels into the room with him. Timmy had no doubt that that luggage was Vince's bag of tricks, his tickle torture toys, his tickly implements that he had told Timmy about over their time of internet chatting...

"Sorry it took me so damned long to find parking," Vince said to Christopher as he held the author tightly in his arms, Christopher massaging the back of Vince's big neck as he spoke. "But Manhattan is not a good place to bring a car..."

"Well, I did manage to kill time while we waited for you," Christopher said with an evil looking grin and pecked Vince on the lips.

"Yeah, and I bet I can guess how the hell you killed time my favorite author," Vince laughed and pressed his lips against Christopher's once more, sniffing at the same time. "Your breath smells like Timmy B. cum...hee, hee, hee..."

At the sound of that "hee, hee, hee" a chill crept up the tied down Timmy's spine and he curled his toes back under his sheer thick and thin silk socks. It was the sound of his tickle tormentor, Tickle Master Vince's trademark sinister chuckle, a simple hee, hee, hee, but mind-bending nonetheless. The handsome laddy wondered what the fuck he had been thinking when he had agreed to all this. He swallowed hard and was treated to a mouth and throat full of his own sock taste, DANG!

"You've been milking that guy for a while huh?" Vince laughed and kissed Christopher again on the lips.

"A few times, yes, it's amazing what a pair of black silk socks, kangaroo pouch undies, tit clamps and a Viagra tablet or two will do for a handsome Southern guy," Christopher said and he and Vince disengaged their embrace.

Christopher gestured conspiratorially over at his tied up prize...

"And there he is, ticklish Timmy B. my handsome ticklish boy!" Vince squealed, shucked off his jacket, tossed it on a chair and with Christopher beside him made his way over to the table that Timmy was stretched out on and tied down to.

"HA, HA, just like I thought my ticklish laddy, just like I said on the phone," Vince said merrily, stepping behind Timmy's head and snaking his long dexterous fingertips through Timmy's soft salt and pepper colored hair. "Tied up, tied down, and wearing just your trademark kangaroo undies, Christopher Trevor black socks and gagged...gagged with one of your own dress socks I would guess...HA, HA, and hee, hee, hee for you my laddy. What a HOT looking display you make buddy..."

"RRRRRMMMFFF..." Timmy panted at Vince's touch, looking up at the guy in a mixture of awe, lust and fear.

As Vince's fingers played over Timmy's handsome face the tickle master leaned down and kissed him on his sock gagged mouth.

"MMMMMM...finally, *finally* my Timmy B. my ticklish laddy, finally, I get to torment you in the flesh..." Vince chuckled as he sidled his way down the side of the table, testing the tightness of the ropes that bound his and Christopher's tickle victim. "And trust me on this Timmy B. I am going to tickle your flesh till you're crazy with it. And look, just look at these ticklish Timmy B. man sized nipples, your man tits as you call them in the book. You guys weren't kidding when you said you had man sized tits Timmy B. Are they really as ticklish as you described in the book?"

"mmmmffff..." was all Timmy could say in response.

Timmy watched miserably as Vince made like an operating room doctor and held up an open hand for Christopher. Christopher smiled wickedly, reached into his pants pocket and brought out two sharp tipped cotton swabs on sticks. The author handed the swabs to Vince.

"Time to do some quick experimenting my ticklish laddy," Vince said as he leered down at his tied up tickle trophy. "God, you're more handsome than your pictures will attest to Laddy..."

As Vince brought the tips of the swabs toward the jutted up tips of Timmy's nipples Timmy shook his head "NO" back and forth and sputtered against his sock gag.

"Been sucking these man sized nipples of his huh Christopher?" Vince asked as he then swirled the tips of the swabs against the tips of Timmy's nipples.

"RRRMMMFFFFFF!" Timmy squawked loudly and Christopher quickly took the sock out of Timmy's mouth.

The author knew never to keep a laughing guy gagged as it ran the risk of him choking.

"PWWWAHHHHHHHH, ha, ha, ha, ha, ha, ha, ha, ha, ha, ha, ha!" Timmy laughed as Vince tickle/swabbed his nipple tips. "And hello to you too Tickle Master Vince! HAHAHAHAHAHAHAHAHAHA!"

The sight of the swab tips being spun over his nipples was unnerving for Timmy and Vince seemed to know just how to spin them and at just the right speed and tempo...

"HAHAHAHAHAHAHAHA, what a way to get started on me, t-ticklin' my danged nips!" Timmy laughed.

"Damn, his Southern accent is sooooo sexy," Vince said to Christopher after he stopped tickling the laddy's nipple tips. "You were so right about this guy..."

"He is a treasure," Christopher said as he and Vince stood at the sides of Timmy's upper torso. "Shall we Vince?"

"Oh yes, those man tits of his are too, *too* irresistible buddy," Vince said breathlessly.

Together, like two vampires Christopher and Vince leaned over the tied up Timmy's chest and helped themselves to one of his nipples each.

"OHHHHHHHHH, oh my word, oh me, oh my..." Timmy grunted breathlessly as his two tickle tormentors made sport of sucking and slurping at his jutted up nipples. "Oh my, for a guy I really have sensitive man nips..."

As Christopher and Vince played suck and slurp with his man tits Timmy's cock and balls churned and he again curled his toes back under his silk socks...

A short while later Vince was strumming his piano player-like fingertips down Timmy's sides, tickling his ribs as he went.

"YAAAA, ha, ha, ha, ha, ha, ha, ha, ha, ha, ha, ha, ha, ha, ha, ha, ha!" Timmy cackled as Vince played Timmy's ribs with his fingertips while Christopher twisted and turned one of his nipples. "Oh you guys, what've I gotten myself into here today?"

"I warned you my handsome laddy, my ticklish Timmy B. I told you that my fingers were lethal tickle weapons," Vince mused. "Did you think I was lying when I said that I took extensive piano lessons when I was a child? Vince strummed his fingertips up and down and up and down all along Timmy's tied down sides and ribs. A few times he leaned down and swirled his thick tongue tip into Timmy's belly button. That really got a few good hee's and haws out of Timmy Backman... To really make the handsome laddy laugh Vince used the tips of his well manicured fingernails to tickle Timmy's sides and ribs. While Vince played Timmy's ribs with his long fingers and fingertips and teased his belly button with his tongue Christopher worked the tied up laddy's nipples with his fingers and thumbs. Timmy laughed and screamed under the binding ropes and his cock flip-flopped from side to side outside his kangaroo pouch under shorts...

"And just think Timmy B. all of this is just a warm-up, a quick experiment for what's coming later..." Vince mused as he trailed his tongue over Timmy's stomach region, kissing him a few times there as he went.

"OH my word, I get the feeling that I'll also be coming later..." Timmy gasped as his cock danced between his legs.

"Our dear author here is going to leave us alone for a while very shortly my ticklish tied up tied down Timmy B.," Vince laughed, looking over at Christopher. "Aren't you buddy?"

Christopher nodded in the affirmative and Timmy laughed louder as Vince did his work...

A few minutes later Vince stopped strumming Timmy's ribs and moved his hands over the sides of the tied up laddy's trademark kangaroo pouch undies, teasing him relentlessly.

"Oh man, just look at that juicy cock Christopher," Vince said sounding totally fiendish. "I would bet that that slit of his is real ticklish..."

"Oh no, oh my word, VINCE, you wouldn't," Timmy panted.

"Unless you want to chew on your sock again I wouldn't say things like that my ticklish laddy," Christopher said, dangling Timmy's navy blue sock over his nose and mouth as Vince took Timmy's balls in hand.

"MMM, nice hefty balls, and even though you've milked this guy a few times they feel like they're chock filled to the rim with his Brim," Vince chuckled, leaned down and slid his tongue liberally over and around Timmy's juicy balls.

"OOOOOOOOOOOOO..." Timmy swooned, arched his head back and goose bumps broke out all over him as Vince's tongue worked its magic.

It was obvious to Timmy how Vince was biding his time in getting to the prize he sought the most...Timmy's tied up feet...Timmy wondered if by the time Vince got to his feet Christopher would have left them alone. The thought of being alone and tied up and in Vince's clutches sent waves of chills of trepidation mixed with longing through Timmy's very being. Vince swirled his huge tongue all over Timmy's balls in their sexy sac. He sucked them alternately into his mouth, bathed them with his saliva and made sure they were well saturated. When he held up his long goose feather Timmy nearly screamed. But then, Timmy did scream, he screamed his laughter as the man he called Tickle Master Vince glided the tip of the feather against his wetted testicles.

"OOOOO, HAHAHAHAHAHAHA!" Timmy laughed loudly, looking up at his author buddy as the guy continued to twist and squeeze his nipples. "HAR, HAR, HAR, HAR, oh my word, Christopher, he, he's tickling my danged scrotum..."

At the sound of the word that Timmy used to describe his sac of balls Vince and Christopher laughed meanly. Vince smiled wickedly down at the tied up guy and trailed his feather upwards against the underside of

Timmy's cock shaft.

"HAHAHAHAHAHAHAHAHAHAHAHAHAHAHAHA!" Timmy reeled.

Christopher watched in awe as Vince worked his sadistic magic on his buddies cock and balls with the feather tip. As the feather strummed against his cock Timmy wanted to plead with Vince to jack him off. After all the times he had been milked by Christopher Timmy could not believe that he was fair game for milking yet again. Jeez, but that Viagra sure could make a guy his age a seventeen year old again Timmy thought fleetingly and laughed and cackled and screeched as Vince clamped the tip of his cock into his lips, pressed down hard and continued tickling the tied up guy's cock shaft. When Vince swirled his tongue tip into Timmy's cock slit while still holding the guy's cock-crown between his lips Timmy felt like he was in orbit...his head was spinning that much and his laughter sounded as if it were coming from someone else...someone very far away... As Vince teased and tickled Timmy the tied up guy heard himself pleading to be allowed to shoot his load...in between laughing raucously that is...

"Got him right where I want him," Vince said after letting the tip of Timmy's cock slip slowly from between lips. "He's totally horned up again...PERFERCT!"

A short while later Timmy was alone with Vince in the hotel room. Christopher had gone out for a while to enjoy the city, leaving his two buddies alone to get to know each other better...or to be more precise and to the point...the author left Timmy and Tickle Master Vince alone so that Vince could reap his tickle magic on the Southern gentleman...

"OH NO, NO," Timmy crowed loudly as Vince took a pair of wooden stocks from his luggage (bag) of tricks.

"I just knew I should have blindfolded you my laddy," Vince said comically as he stood at the foot of the table.

He slowly untied Timmy's socked feet and then one at a time de-socked the executive.

"I know how much Christopher loves seeing you in your black socks buddy," Vince said as he dropped the socks to the floor. "But for what I have in store for you now requires you to be sock less..."

"OH MY, Vince, please, oh please man, don't lock my feet in those danged stocks," Timmy panted. "Please man, I'm so worked up from the

Viagra and from being tickled and from the way Christopher milked me and from having had my man tits clamped off and on that I'm afraid I'll laugh so hard I'll make the ceiling fly off this place…OH ME…"

"Just what I'm hoping for my ticklish prince," Vince replied as Timmy prattled in the throes of ticklish ecstasy and set the stocks down at the foot of the table between Timmy's splayed legs.

"Oh no," Timmy whimpered as he watched Vince then encase each of his feet in the stocks at his ankles.

The bottoms of Timmy's soft meaty feet protruded through the stocks and his toes stuck straight up as he lay atop the table, feeling totally helpless and very sexy and very ticklish. The sounds of the stocks being closed and locked filled Timmy with the utmost dread…

"Now my laddy, lets see AND HEAR just how loud I can make you laugh and HAR HAR HAR for me, yes?" Vince asked his ticklish captive while at the same time reaching into his bag of tricks.

"Yes? Why, no, no Vince," Timmy pleaded miserably, cursing himself for having come to New York City in the first place.

When Vince held up the electronic manicure buffer Timmy nearly started laughing involuntarily. When Vince clicked the device on and the buzzing sound filled the hotel room Timmy nearly started crying…

With a maniacal looking grin on his face, with his pearly white teeth gleaming Vince stood at the foot of the table, at Timmy's bared feet in the stocks…

"Oh my laddy, prepare to go to the city of sadistic laughter now…" Vince said and with no hesitation whatsoever pressed the rotating tip of the manicure buffer against the bottom of Timmy's right foot.

"OH NOOOOO, NOOOO, OHHHHH WOE is me and my danged ticklish feet!" Timmy screamed. "HAHAHAHAHAHAHAHA! HAAAAAAAAAAA! VINCE, stop this, how about at least buying a guy a drink first before de-socking and ticking his danged feet? HAAAAAAAAAAAAA!"

As Vince swirled the innocent looking manicure buffer over Timmy's right foot and then his left foot Timmy thought of his wife Stephanie and how many times he had gone to meet her in the salon after she'd been for her bi-weekly manicure. When he saw the row of ladies having their nails done, some of them having their nails done with the electronic manicure device he never once entertained thoughts of that sort of device being used on his ticklish bare feet...

"OHHHHHHH, if Stephanie could see me now," Timmy cackled crazily. "HAR, HAR, HAR, HAR, HAR, HAR, HAR, HAR, HAR!"

Vince watched with awe and his eyes opened nearly as wide as saucers as Timmy's beautiful feet flopped around in the stocks as they were tickle tortured. The tickle master would never be able to thank Christopher enough for having brought Timmy Backman to him in the flesh. After a good (bad?) half hour or so of having his bare feet tickled with the manicure buffer Timmy was sweating and panting atop the table as Vince released his feet from the stocks.

"I'll get you some cool water buddy," Vince said, sounding concerned.

But when Vince took the leather restraints and bindings from his bag of tricks Timmy wondered just how concerned the guy really was... GAWD...

A few moments later Timmy was finally off the massage table. Standing next to Vince with his wrists now locked behind him in leather wrist restraints Timmy slowly sipped the water from the bottle that Vince was holding to his lips. Vince marveled at the way Timmy's Adam's apple bobbed up and down as he gulped down the cool liquid. Actually, Vince was marveling over every part of this overly handsome overly ticklish guy. Timmy Backman was a tickle sadist's dream come true. Vince wondered how poor Timmy would feel if he knew that the water he was chugging down was laced with crushed up Viagra tablets. Actually, the ticklish guy would know very soon... He had been begging to be allowed to cum earlier while Vince was tickle torturing him. Now Vince could not wait to hear the guy plead in true earnest...

"So tell me Laddy, when was the last time you were hogtied with your bare sexy feeties pointing straight up while a diabolical guy like me lick tickled those said feet?" Vince asked his tickle captive.

As Timmy sputtered at what Vince just asked him Vince grabbed his arm and laughed sadistically...

The water trailed down the sides of Timmy's chin as Vince held him tight by the arm and forced him to scoff down the liquid...

"What all did you put in that danged water?" Timmy asked Vince a short while later when he was hogtied in the leather restraints on the hotel room bed.

By now Timmy was totally naked, seeing as Vince had taken his kangaroo pouch style underpants off him, telling Timmy he was taking them as a souvenir of this wonderful ticklish experience.

"Ticklish experience for me but not for you oh Tickle Master Vince," Timmy had cawed as he was de-under-pantsed.

"Are we feeling a bit worked up in the crotch my ticklish Timmy B.?" Vince asked his tickle hostage as Timmy now squirmed miserably in his hogtied position on the bed, his bare feet pointing straight up at the ceiling.

To tease the restrained guy all the more Vince stuck his long tongue out and swirled it seductively over his lips and near his prickly looking goatee.

"Oh my word," Timmy said softly as thoughts of that tongue and goatee tickling his bare feet filled him with dread. "But yes, I am feeling real worked up in my root man!"

"Amazing what a small dose of that Viagra can do to a guy eh Timmy my laddy?" Vince asked in reply and reached between Timmy's thighs from behind.

He pulled Timmy's sensitive feeling and bloated cock from between his thighs, along with his balls. Timmy's most private of parts flopped onto the bed and trickled pre seed.

"OH MY," Timmy cried out at Vince's touch on his cock. "You tricked me into drinking water laced with that damned sex potion that Christopher was giving me as well. Milking me like a cow, making me cum repeatedly just makes me all the more ticklish...but then I suppose that is what you guys would want where I'm concerned...OH MY WORD..."

Then, poor Timmy was off and laughing again as Vince licked and tickled his bare feet with his tongue and ran the prickly parts of his goatee over Timmy's feet as well. With his hand Vince reached down with his goose feather and tickled Timmy's visible cock and balls as they peeked out from between his tethered thighs...

"OHHHHHH! HAHAHAHAHAHAHAHAHAHA!" Timmy reeled and cackled. "I for one cannot believe that Christopher left me here alone with you man!"

"Keep talking in that Southern Senator John Edwards voice for me my laddy," Vince said. "It makes me want to tickle you all the more...and more...and more..."

As his feet and cock and balls were tickled Timmy wriggled like a fish out of water in his hogtied position. Vince was in awe once again as Timmy's delectable toes curled back and forth as he stuck the tip of the feather into his cock slit...

Timmy laughed in a high-pitched tone as Vince nibbled at his toes and kissed the sides of his feet, all the while using his goatee to tickle torture the guy's feet.

"HAHAHAHAHAHAHA!" Timmy roared and wondered if he would survive the weekend in Christopher Trevor and Tickle Master Vince's clutches...

Then Vince switched tactics and used his goose feather to tickle torture the bottoms of Timmy's upturned feet with...

Timmy heee hawed and cackled and swore like a sailor as he laughed and laughed and laughed.... When Vince started sucking Timmy's toes one after the other while at the same time tickling his feet bottoms with the tip of the goose feather the Southern guy was bathed in a mixture of laughter and marvelous sexual sensations in his cock. Having his toes sucked always made the guy's cock hard. It seemed that like with his man-sized nipples, when they were played just right it affected the handsome laddy in the cock.

"I-I got, I got to cum, oh Tickle Master Vince, I REALLY got to cum..." Timmy cried out in between bouts of laughter. "HAHAHAHAHAHAHAHAHA! My cock feels like it's stalked up to the size of gargantuan...HAHAHAHAHAHAHAHA!"

A surge of emotion akin to high lust flooded through Vince's being as he heard Timmy call him by his rightful title of "Tickle Master." This told him that inwardly Timmy loved the role he was playing...even though he somehow hated (and loved?) being tickle tortured. Vince decided that throughout the weekend ahead he would work the laddy harder and harder. Smiling with two of Timmy's small toes in his mouth Vince sucked those toes hard and tickled the arches of the Southerner's restrained feet. As Timmy laughed and laughed and laughed his feet bobbed around beautifully in the leather restraints...

After an hour or so of tickling Timmy's feet with the goose feather, licking them and tickling them goatee-wise and sucking his toes Vince decided that the guy had suffered enough...for the moment. As he was releasing Timmy from the hogtie was when Christopher sauntered back into the hotel room.

"Anybody hungry?" Christopher asked. "I made dinner reservations for us down in the hotel's beautiful dining room."

"Sounds good to me," Vince said as he and Christopher watched the sexy Southern Timmy sit up on the bed, massaging his wrists and each of the men noticing the size of the stalk between the handsome laddy's legs.

"Oh yes, sure, dinner sounds like a very good plan," Timmy said breathlessly. "After all the tickling and milking that you two have done to me thus far I sure could use some nourishment..."

"Hmm, I see you stripped him of his socks and underpants," Christopher said as Vince sidled up next to his buddy.

"Yeah, I wanted those sexy feeties of his bare for my tickling tortures," Vince mused.

"So the hotel dining room sounds good to me..." Timmy said, getting to his feet and standing there naked and stalked up real sexy in the cock.

Christopher and Vince looked hungrily at the towering erection and low hanging testicles that the sweaty and tickled guy was sporting between his muscular legs. Timmy chuckled knowingly as Christopher picked up a pair of Vince's leather wrist restraints...

"HEH, heh, looks like dinner is going to be a tad delayed me thinks," Timmy said as Christopher yanked his arms behind him and cinched his wrists in the leather cuffs.

A few moments later Timmy was standing with his hands locked behind him in the leather cuffs as Christopher and Vince knelt at his sides sucking on his balls.

"OHHHHHHH, oh my, oh my word..." Timmy bantered breathlessly. "OH my, ticklers love my sweaty and mangy balls...can't wait till you two take sucking turns on my beet red cock down there..."

Timmy balanced himself on his bare feet and as he spoke in his Southern sounding accent it seemed that Vince sucked his testicle that he had in his mouth even harder.

Timmy hunched his muscular shoulders up, his eyes spun back in his head and his breath came in short gasps as his two tickle buddies licked, sucked and lapped at his balls. The ticklish guy hauled himself to his tiptoes and danced sexily as his balls were serviced most lovingly. Then, looking down he watched as Christopher and Vince seemed to really be tugging at his balls while they each held one in their mouths.

"OHHHHH, thanks for not blindfolding me for this Christopher," Timmy swooned, "I just wish you would get to the gusto and suck me off... you know how much you love the taste of my cum buddy..."

Looking up at Timmy Christopher squeezed the laddy's calf, shook his head "no" and let Timmy's testicle slip out of his mouth.

"WH-what no?" Timmy grunted as Vince also let his testicle slip out of his mouth.

"I think it best that I don't ruin my appetite before dinner," Christopher said snidely and stood up next to Timmy, taking the laddy's upper arm in a firm grip.

As Vince got to his feet as well Timmy looked at him expectantly.

"Don't look at me for that my laddy," Vince laughed and tweaked one of Timmy's jutted up nipples.

A chill sped through Timmy's being at Vince's touch and his well sucked and dangling balls seemed to sway in their sac.

"Your buddy Christopher here holds the warrant on drinking down your sludge," Vince laughed.

"I'll have your slop for dessert when me and Vince get back from dinner," Christopher said and let go of Timmy's arm, quickly helping himself to a few more sets of leather restraints from Vince's bag of tricks.

"B-but I thought that the three of us were all going down to the hotel's dining room to eat together," Timmy said, his heart thudding in his muscular chest, him knowing very well the antics that Christopher and Vince would plan for him.

He cursed himself for having let the author bind his hands behind him while having his balls stimulated. Christopher knew just how to play him, DOUBLE DAMN! He knew he was not going to be made to cum at the moment...rather he was going to be made to wait...

"Change of plans my handsome ticklish buddy," Christopher said and then pointed at Vince.

Vince smiled fiendishly, scooped Timmy up off the floor and carried him in a position of a groom carrying his bride over a threshold over to the king-sized bed...

"Oh my word..." Timmy said sounding very frustrated at this latest development.

"Not to worry Timmy, we'll bring you back something from the hotel dining room," Christopher said and then he and Vince went to work overpowering and getting their ticklish captive secured to the bed...

"OH MAN, this is so not fair," Timmy huffed miserably as his wrists were released but then his arms pulled to the sides so that he could be restrained to the bed in a spread eagle position.

"And just think you handsome ticklish guy, the weekend hasn't even gotten started yet, all of this today was a warm-up to what we have in store for you," Christopher said as he cinched Timmy's left wrist to the bed board while Vince did the same with his right wrist.

Timmy looked from side to side as he was restrained.

"So, so you plan to leave me here all tethered and fettered while you both go for a nice leisurely dinner?" Timmy seethed, balling his hands into fists as his two buddies then got to work restraining his bare feet.

By now Timmy was laying on his back and his cock was hard and sticking straight up at the ceiling.

"We won't be gone that long buddy," Christopher said and when he and Vince were done Timmy was spread eagled on the bed, restrained tightly in leather wrist and ankle restraints.

After Christopher and Vince were gone Timmy tried to get as comfortable as possible but given the position he was in that was easier said than done.

"Dang, I can't believe they left me here like this," Timmy mumbled as he squirmed on the bed, his cock doing a dance between his spread legs.

But as he lay there he did find himself nodding off after a while. Timmy was exhausted to the point that eventually he fell into a deep sleep. He had been tickled that day at the airport and by his buddies Christopher and Vince. He had also been milked/drained to the point that only tickling him would more than likely bring him out of his slumber. The ticklish guy actually passed out...spread eagled to the four corners of the bed, naked as the day he was born...not even a pair of trademark "Christopher Trevor" black socks to wear at the moment. And because of all the sexual teasing, stimulation and the strong and constant doses of Viagra Timmy's cock was once again chock filled with his manly juices, rigid and standing tall. The height to which his cock was erect was accentuated by the flatness of his naked body splayed out on the bed.

When Christopher and Vince had left the room, as an afterthought and thinking it would be fiendishly funny Vince hung the "Room Service Please" sign on the doorknob. He giggled like a schoolgirl and pointed Christopher's attention to the sign as they walked away. Christopher also giggled...mostly at the prospects of Timmy being discovered by room service...whoever that might turn out to be.

As Timmy slept the tickle CO-author and tickle victim was lost to time. He was literally dead to world as he slept off the ticklish, teasing torments he had been put through for most of that day. So, he was totally unaware of the passage of time or that a floor manager had spotted the "Room Service" request sign and had alerted housekeeping of a job that needed to be performed. The request was answered promptly, because prompt service was a hallmark of the "Grand Diamond" hotel. A cute little Philippine maid in her crisp black and white uniform came bustling down the hall with her tool cart and entered the room using her master card key with no hesitation.

Once in the room she began to survey the situation to see what she needed to accomplish. She immediately saw that the room was a mess... clothes and stuff strewn all over. She even noted the crumpled pair of black sheer thick and thin dress socks. She instantly thought of a groom occupying this room. She swore under her breath, a new American custom she had picked up during her time in the states and headed to the bathroom to see what damage there might be there. As she trudged angrily through the spaciously large room she suddenly spied the sleeping form on the bed...a naked man...and from quick observation she saw that he was in a state of extreme sexual agitation. His male member was standing tall in the dim light of the room and it was swaying and pulsing with his rhythmic breathing. Slowly, the maid walked up to the bed to examine the handsome naked gringo, this naked American...she nearly lost her breath at the sight of the beautiful form laid out before her.

She noticed that he was obviously and very much alive...because she was able to hear his deep breathing and she loved watching the rise and fall of his muscular chest. He had nipples that were as thick as a woman's she thought. Her boyfriend would go crazy as he was a tit sucker to the extreme. Her own nipples tingled as she thought that. The maid also found that she was salivating a bit as she watched the gentle sway of his huge erect cock as he breathed. She moved down to his bare feet, touched his toe and said, "Sir?" Timmy did not stir. She grabbed more of the toe and squeezed, once more saying "Sir?" There was still no reaction from the sleeping nude man laid out before her. She then took note of the fact that his arms and legs were tied to the bed, pulling his limbs out in a spread eagle position. She also noticed all the paraphernalia scattered about the naked man and on the floor...feathers, brushes, pens, electric toothbrushes and the like. She noticed also an open bottle of pills. She picked up the bottle. The maid knew what Viagra was. She placed the bottle back on the nightstand where several of the blue pills were laying on the surface next to a pitcher of water.

"This is all so bizarre," the maid said to herself. "What in the world has been going on here?"

This time she jostled the naked man's foot. Timmy still did not react. He was still sleeping in an exhausted state. Then, the Philippine maid decided that she just had to call her cousin who also just happened to work this housekeeping shift at the hotel. Using the room phone she called her cousin's cell phone and told the young lady that she would not believe what she had found in this room...and for her to get there right away.

While she waited for her cousin to arrive the maid could not resist kissing Timmy's handsome face a few times and running her fingers in his soft and so sexy salt and pepper colored hair.

Shortly, the other Philippine maid arrived at Timmy's and Christopher's room and she was initially aghast at what she saw. Her cousin seated on the edge of the hotel room bed with a handsome, muscular, naked man tied to the four corners of said bed. Not to mention that his obviously excited cock was sticking straight up but with an angry red look to it.

"Milly!" was the only intelligible word spoken.

The rest was in Philippine.

"Lindy!" the first maid called back and then offered her own Philippine chatter to the mix.

Milly spoke, pointed and gestured at the naked, bound Timmy sleeping on the bed. Lindy chattered back and picked up a couple of the brushes. Then, as if part of her explanation Milly wiggled her bright red fingernails on Timmy's bare sole.

For the first time since Milly entered the room Timmy stirred and mumbled, "No, no! Christopher, no, stop, Vince, no...you can't...please stop." Then, his eyes popped open and he giggled. Timmy continued to giggle as Milly strummed his wrinkled wiggling soles with her sharp nails.

"WHAT...WHO the hell? Who...Don't...hee, hee, hee, hee!" Timmy found himself saying as he struggled with this new and twisted turn of events.

Milly continued to tickle Timmy's foot closest to her and chatting in Philippine to her cousin. The cousin, Lindy, sat on the other side of the bed and grinning meanly she began using her nails on Timmy's other foot. Timmy's eyes were as a big as saucers as he took in the situation. GAWD, he had been found naked and bound on a hotel room bed by two beautiful and obviously very playfully sadistic maids. As his eyes opened wider yet the poor laddy giggled to the beat of the band. He could not seem to communicate with these two very beautiful Philippine maids.

At that point the door to the room opened and the floor manager stepped into the room. Although dressed in blue blazer, tan slacks and shirt and tie she was also obviously of the Philippine descent.

"Milly, Lindy!" she called the two maids by name and then launched into what could be nothing other than an inquisitive tirade.

Even Timmy was looking at the floor manager. His laughter subsided as the two maid's attention had been focused away from him. The maid's chattered back and forth in their native dialect. Now Timmy began asking the floor manager for help. She quickly moved to the bed beside Timmy's head still chattering back and forth with the maids. Seemingly having heard enough from Timmy she clamped her hand firmly over his mouth. Timmy's eyes were still pleading with her however.

A little more chatter and then the floor manager looked back at Timmy.

"Sir, may I ask how you came to be like this...in this ticklish predicament?" she asked and she had to giggle herself at what was in front of her and what the maids had told her.

"Please, help me," Timmy pleaded as soon as her hand was off his mouth. "These two friends...no, guys, er, they kidnapped me. Yes, they kidnapped me and tied me to this bed. And they have been doing awful things to me..."

Timmy tried to sound as convincing as possible; wanting to be untied so he could at least jack himself off when the maids were gone... seeing as their only interest in him seemed to be to want to tickle him.

"Well Sir," the floor manager began and her hand reached out and began to move across Timmy's washboard abs. "This room seems to be registered to a Timothy Backman and Christopher Trevor. And from what my staff tells me they have checked out your wallet and you seem to be Timothy Backman. So, how could your friends kidnap you, hmm?" And her hand moved lower on Timmy's abdomen and her nails began to toy with his pubic hairs above his cock. Timmy giggled as her hand moved across his abs and he moaned as she found his pubic bush and toyed with his hair...his stiff cock lurched and began to leak. The steady diet of Viagra that Christopher had been feeding him had left Timmy in a constant state of overly sensitive, sexual excitement. His cock needed very little stimulation to begin oozing the clear, sticky substance everyone knew as a guy's "Pre-cum."

"OH, oh maam, please! Uh, well it may...oh...oh...it may be my room and the gentleman you just mentioned, Christopher Trevor's as well, but please, you're not helping...don't...please maam..." Timmy blubbered, trying to explain himself and get her to stop what she was doing.

Christopher and Vince had tickled and teased and drained his balls over and over...and yet...he was responding to this woman's teasing...and she really wasn't even touching his cock...just playing in his pubic hair.

The maid Milly chimed in but in Philippine. The floor manager was still toying with Timmy's pubic hair interpreted for him.

"Milly thinks that you have been subjected to quite a bit of tickling," the floor manager said and pointed out all the paraphernalia lying around the room. "Is that right Mr. Backman, hmm? And as Milly the maid picked up a battery powered toothbrush that she found near Vince's bag of tricks

Timmy moaned again and responded, "Huh? OH mmm, oh! What?" as the floor manager was still stroking his pubic hair, pulling at it to make him feel it in his erection and sweaty balls. But when Milly began to comb Timmy's armpit hair with the buzzing vibrating device Timmy's reaction was abrupt and violent. He leapt right from moaning to full nose blowing giggles.

"Eeeeeeeeeeee hee, hee, hee, heee HEEEE! PLEEAASSE hee, hee, hee, hee, heee! Don't tickle me anymore! EEEEEEEEEEE!" Timmy screamed shrilly.

Milly continued her toothbrush tickling of Timmy's armpit and jabbered to the floor manager. The floor manager responded, "Yes, I too think that the size of his erection does indicate that Mr. Backman here really enjoys this tickling activity. Don't you Sir?"

"EEEEEEEeeeeeeeeeeee hee, hee, heee, ha, ha, ha, ha, ha, ha, ha, ha OOOOOOOO, hoo, hoo, hoo, hoo, hoo, hoo!" was all the response she got out of Timmy.

Then, the other maid, Lilly, not wanting to be left out of this sexy tickling action picked up a ballpoint pen and began to draw all kinds of designs on poor Timmy's bare soles. Timmy's response was repetitive...but at a little higher pitch.

"EEEEEEE, HEEEE, HEEE, HEEEE, HEE HAHAHAHAHA, ha, ha, ha, ha, ha, ha, ha, ha, ha, ha!" was what Timmy screamed.

And all the while the Southern laddy's cock remained stiff and leaking and his balls rumbled in their sack. Timmy never could control his sexual response to being tickled. And even though Christopher and Vince had spent a great deal of time tickling and draining him Timmy was still full of Viagra and threatening to blow his cork yet again. So, while Milly and Lilly enjoyed tickling Timmy's armpits and feet...they even switched places and switched instruments...the floor manager found an electric toothbrush of her own. It was amazing how much Vince's bag of tricks contained. She held it up in the air and tested it out...but, Timmy never heard the buzz. He never saw the evil gleam in her eye... He never saw the second toothbrush coming...But, he felt it.

The floor manager started out on Timmy's perineum. Timmy's eyes popped open and his breath left his lungs in a wheeze. She moved up and found his rumbling ball sac and buzzed his filling nuts...driving him closer and closer to becoming a nut. The floor manager was literally having a ball. Grinning, she moved the buzzing bristles around Timmy's balls...playing along the stretched tendons in his crotch, up through his pubic hair and then up and around his pulsing shaft. Timmy's cock was no longer the dry rod it had started out to be. Now it had a generous coating of pre cum, which was still pulsing out of his piss slit.

Timmy was howling and laughing and pleading, "OOOOOHHHHH PPLLEEEASE", and going crazy... Then, the floor manager began to work the vibrating toothbrush up the underside of Timmy's wet stiff cock. He was beside himself with laughter and lust as the three lovelies handled and used and tickled the daylights out of him. The floor manager worked the brush closer and closer to the head of Timmy's erection. She skirted the edge of the mushroom head...she even gave his piss slit a good vibrating...and the she slipped the buzzing bristles down his cock head and found the sweet spot where his cock shaft and cock head met with a little tuft of loose skin...and she brushed and vibrated this spot good. And she was rewarded with an explosion of cum and Timmy's nuts drew up and started pumping his man juice out once again...only this time Christopher was not there to scoff it down.

Just at that moment, as Timmy was spurting the last of his sexy mess all over himself the three women stopped tickling him and turned to meet the sound at the hotel room door. Timmy was still giggling and slightly squirting white gooey cum onto his chest and face as the door to the room opened. When the door swung open there stood the two Cheshire cats that had put poor Timmy in this predicament...Christopher and Vince. Christopher was holding a bag that contained Timmy's take-out dinner from the hotel dining room. The two men clucked their tongues and Vince was the first to speak as he said, "Well, well, well, it looks like Timmy couldn't wait for us and decided to call room service." Timmy looked at them miserably in his exhausted state as Christopher and Vince laughed and laughed. They thanked the floor manager and her maids for tending to the room and to Timmy while they were out. Christopher told her that they could handle it from here. As the women left Timmy was still wearing the freakish grin of a Halloween Jack-o-lantern...and he had a fresh coating of his cum dripping from his nose and chin. The women closed the door amid the chuckles of the two men as they took charge of the very ticklish handsome man they had found bound to the bed...

Before they un-tethered Timmy so that he could eat his dinner Vince came up with a ticklish idea for the poor laddy. Timmy found himself bent over in an upside down "U" shape position. His wrists were now bound to his ankles and as he balanced himself awkwardly in that position Vince used an electric toothbrush to tickle torment Timmy's exposed asshole from his standing position beside Timmy. In back of Timmy Christopher amused himself sucking the ticklish guy's cock...after he had squeezed the spent member through the crack of Timmy's muscular and shapely thighs...

"OH MY WORD, oh me, HAHAHAHAHAHAHAHA!" Timmy cackled as his two captors tormented him all the more.

Timmy's spent cock tingled as Christopher sucked it heartily. He did not cum that time but before he sat down to eat his dinner he was given a Viagra appetizer... For Timmy Backman that night proved to be the prelude to a very long and ticklish weekend of ticklish trials...

Epilogue

The weekend was at a close and Timmy Backman had survived yet another ticklish ordeal... As the cab he was in headed for the "Village Bookstore" on late Sunday afternoon the handsome and suited executive wondered just how the "Christopher Trevor" display at the bookstore would look. All during being tickle tortured while in Christopher and Vince's clutches the bookstore and the "new Ronald" were all Timmy could think about. Well, the bookstore wasn't actually all he thought about. He also thought about how long his two buddies/tormentors would tickle torture him during the intervals they had him tied up. But it was while he was not being tickled and not laughing his head off that he thought about the "new Ronald" and his bookstore. As the weekend drew to a close and his two so called buddies finally released him (rather reluctantly it seemed, seeing as Christopher sucked one last load from Timmy's cock while his hands were still tied behind him) Timmy called for a cab to pick him up earlier than when he was supposed to head for the airport. He never told Christopher and Vince about the "new Ronald", wanting this to be something for him and for *him only*...So many times now in his real life and his fictional life he had been the tickle victim and catered to the needs of so many other's, so this time he wanted an experience that would not result in his being captured and tickle tortured. This time it would be for his own enjoyment Timmy mused delightedly as he rode in the cab, tugging his tie. According to the business card that "Ronald Rosalie" had given him the name of the bookstore was aptly "The Village Bookstore." It was located on a side street in the heart of the west side of Greenwich Village. He had called ahead to let the "new Ronald" know that he would be stopping by before having to head off to the airport and back to Georgia. Shortly, the cab pulled up in front of the "Village Bookstore" and Timmy, clad spiffily in a charcoal colored suit, a white shirt, black silk tie and black lace-up wingtips emerged from the cab, carrying his one piece of luggage with him. He paid the driver and as the cab drove off and he approached the door to the store the first thing the handsome Southern gentleman noticed was the sign hanging on the inside of the door that read, "Closed." Timmy wondered if perhaps "Ronald Rosalie" had had an emergency of some sort and had to run off. But as he was about to step away from the store the door opened and there stood the "new Ronald."

"Timmy, so glad you could make it to come and see my store," Ronald Rosalie said happily, standing in the archway of the entrance to the establishment.

"Oh, Ronald, hey there," Timmy said and held out a hand.

The two men shook hands vigorously, Ronald really pumping Timmy's hand.

"The sign on the door said "Closed" so I thought maybe our meeting had been called off," Timmy said as Ronald continued holding his hand after they had stopped shaking.

"Nah, well, yeah, I closed the store so we could have some privacy Timmy," Ronald said and finally let go of Timmy's hand. "Come on in, put that luggage under the front counter and I'll show you around."

"Thanks, sounds good to me," Timmy said and stepped into the store.

"Can I get you something? A coffee perhaps? I have a café area in the store as well," Ronald said as Timmy slid his luggage under the counter in the very front of the store. "I find that a lot of customers like to sit and sip a coffee after they purchase a book or two. This way they can get right into the story they bought..."

"Uh sure, a coffee sounds good Ronald, thanks," Timmy replied. "A little bit of skim milk, no sugar please."

"Coming right up Timmy," Ronald said and sauntered over to the area of the store where a sign hung over it that read "Village Bookstore Café."

While Ronald was preparing his coffee Timmy slid his hands into his suit pants pockets and looked around the place, moving slowly on his feet.

"Nice, nice place," Timmy said as he took in the rows and rows and shelves of books.

Like most bookstores each section was properly marked with a hanging sign over it, whether it was fiction, non-fiction, horror, romance, etc...

"Timmy stepped over to the section marked "Fiction" but did not find a row of the "Christopher Trevor" books.

"Here you go Timmy," Ronald said, startling Timmy a bit as he made him come out of his reverie.

"Oh, thanks, thanks a lot, it smells great," Timmy said, taking the medium sized container of coffee from his new friend, the "new Ronald" to be exact. "Say uh, nice store you have here Ronald, but I don't see the display of "Christopher Trevor" books anywhere."

"I have them in a section in back of the store," the "new Ronald" said with a sly looking grin on his face. "It's for adults only. I have a sign posted at the front counter that says you must be eighteen years of age or older in order to shop the "Christopher Trevor" section of the store."

"Yes, when customers order books from Christopher he insists on a letter stating that the customer is eighteen years or older," Timmy said and sipped his coffee. "Well, I can assure you Ronald, I am very well over eighteen years of age so please lead the way to the "Christopher Trevor" display of books."

The two men laughed good naturedly at Timmy's comment concerning his age...

"Wait till you see what else I have back there Timmy," the "new Ronald" said and pulled a long white handkerchief from his pocket. "You are going to be bowled over when you see this. Do you mind if I blindfold you for a few moments?"

Timmy breathed a sigh as the "new Ronald" without hesitation and without a reply from Timmy stepped behind him and tied the white cloth over the handsome laddy's eyes.

"Hold that coffee steady Timmy," the "new Ronald" said and guided Timmy by holding him by his upper arms toward the back part of the store. "I assure you, you are going to be amazed."

"Well, seeing as you blindfolded me for it I'm sure I will be," Timmy said and managed a chuckle.

He felt a tingle in his cock as he was led in darkness toward the back of the store... Holding Timmy's arms tight the "new Ronald" led the suited handsome guy through a door at the rear of the store.

"Okay, here we are Timmy," the "new Ronald" stated happily.

The "new Ronald" positioned Timmy facing the display and then put his fingers on the knot in his blindfold.

"You ready?" the "new Ronald" asked.

"I'm ready Sir," Timmy said and as the blindfold was whipped off him he took a hearty sip of his coffee.

Timmy could not believe what he saw...

The entire section at the back of the store was decorated and adorned ala "Christopher Trevor." Over a shelf of rows of "Christopher Trevor" books the "new Ronald" had hung a poster-sized portrait of the author himself. Timmy recognized the picture of Christopher as his author photo from the books. Around the poster of Christopher were poster-sized pictures of the covers of all of Christopher Trevor's books. Looking up Timmy saw the cover of "Timmy's Ticklish Trials." He smiled widely, took a sip of his coffee and his cock tingled more in his suit pants.

"Oh my word," Timmy said in awe as the "new Ronald" stood beside him, gloweringly thrilled that Timmy Backman was enjoying this. "I feel like a celebrity of sorts..."

But it was what was situated on the side of the shelf of books that truly mesmerized Timmy. It was an exact replica of the one he and Stephanie had at home, the dreaded device called...

"...the Spinning Chinaman," Timmy said softly and in wonder as he took a final sip of his coffee.

"Yep, the Spinning Chinaman," the "new Ronald" said as Timmy put his empty coffee cup down on an empty spot on the bookshelf and with his cock now at full mast in his suit pants he approached the device. "One of the many instruments of your ticklish tortures Timmy Backman."

"Oh my word, wherever did you get this?" Timmy asked as the "new Ronald" sidled up next to him.

"As you can see I have read the "Timmy" books very carefully," the "new Ronald" stated. I plan to even get a shoe shine machine with the tickly brushes in it to add to the other side of the bookshelf."

Timmy looked at the "new Ronald" out of the side of his vision, smiled thinly and tugged nervously at his tie.

"Did uh, did Valerie from the stories sell you this Chinaman?" Timmy asked as he took in the huge wheel-shaped device, complete with the leather restraints for wrists and ankles adorning it, the pin in the center in place to keep it from rotating at the moment.

"No, that would be funny though if she did," the "new Ronald" replied and saw the erection tenting Timmy's suit pants, but made no mention of it however. "Actually I had a buddy of mine build it from scratch. I had him read the Timmy books and he made it from the way it was described in the story."

"Well, I must say, whoever your buddy is he really got it down pat," Timmy said, running a hand over the side of the huge wheel. "...even down to the finest details..."

As the two men took in the sight of the device the "new Ronald's" eyes opened wide and he smiled from ear to ear.

"Timmy, I have a brilliant idea, if you're game for it that is," the "new Ronald" said and grasped Timmy's upper arm.

"I uh, think I know what you're about to say Ronald," Timmy said with a grin, his erection pounding now in his suit pants, it leading the way and his thoughts it seemed at that point.

"How about some pictures of you in the "Spinning Chinaman" Timmy?" Ronald asked and squeezed Timmy's arm tighter, coaxing him along it seemed. "It would be great publicity for sales of the "Timmy" books." Timmy slid his hands into his suit pants pockets and grinned like a schoolboy.

"I don't know Ronald," Timmy said. "I have a plane to catch and all and..." Timmy began.

"It would take no time, just get yourself standing in the device for a few minutes, I'll snap the pictures and then you'll be headed for the airport," the "new Ronald" said hopefully.

"Hmmm, okay, I suppose that sounds reasonable and all," Timmy said as the "new Ronald" loosened his grip on his arm. "As long as the pictures would only be shown here and not posted on the internet or anything like that...I am a family man after all..."

"Of course Timmy, I'll even draw up an agreement paper, sort of like a contract," the "new Ronald" said. "How does that sound?"

Timmy considered it, clapped his hands together once and said, "It sounds like a good deal Ronald Rosalie."

"I'll get the camera, you get yourself comfortable in the Chinaman," Ronald said and headed for the door of the room they were in. "I'll be back in less than a minute."

"You uh, you'll want me in my under shorts and trademark black socks I'm guessing?" Timmy asked as he was undoing his tie and the "new Ronald" halted in his steps.

The store owner could not believe his luck...

He dashed to the front counter to get his camera and when he returned to the "Christopher Trevor" display room Timmy was shirtless and just taking off his suit pants. His shoes had been placed by the bookshelf and his suit jacket and shirt and tie were hung neatly over the shelf.

"Nice, looks like you workout pretty regularly," the "new Ronald" said as he took in the sight of Timmy in his kangaroo pouch under shorts and black calf length nylon dress socks. "That will make the pictures even better..."

What would make the pictures truly great thought the "new Ronald" was the towering erection that Timmy Backman was sporting in his trademark under shorts. If Timmy hadn't figured out that the coffee he had just drunk was laced with a powerful aphrodisiac he would know soon enough...when the "new Ronald" started edging him that is... As the "new Ronald" put his camera down momentarily he stepped next to Timmy to usher him into the "Spinning Chinaman."

"Okay Timmy, just get yourself situated in there like in the story and I'll get the pictures taken as quickly as possible," the "new Ronald" said as Timmy positioned himself in an "X" sort of stance within the device, his arms and legs spread out as far as possible.

"Okay, how's that?" Timmy asked, looking real sexy and vulnerable already.

"So far so good," the "new Ronald" said as he stood next to the Chinaman and quickly fastened the restraint around one of Timmy's wrists.

"Oh, uh, I didn't think you would tether me to it," Timmy said and as he reached to release himself the "new Ronald" grabbed his other wrist from the other side of the Chinaman, having made his way over there at almost lightning-like speed.

In moments both of Timmy's wrists were fastened to the dreaded "Spinning Chinaman."

"I just want it to look as authentic as possible Timmy," the "new Ronald" said as he then squatted at Timmy's black socked feet.

As the "new Ronald" pulled Timmy's black socks up for him it was at that moment that all the warning signals went off in his head...and "OH MY WORD" it was too late yet again... His big cock churned and stiffened in fear in his under shorts as the "new Ronald" handled his black socks, pulling them up for him, straightening them about his muscular sexy calves... As he watched the "new Ronald" handling his socks thoughts of his other buddy Ronald Greene flitted through the handsome laddy's mind. Thoughts of what that original Ronald had subjected him to filled his tortured brain and his cock churned some more...OH MY WORD...

Timmy did not need three guesses to know what this "new Ronald" had in store for him as he fastened the restraints around his socked ankles...

"Okay, now *that* looks great Timmy my laddy, that looks really great," the "new Ronald said almost breathlessly as he took in the sight of the now scantily clad and bonded Timmy. "And I'm glad you left your black socks on, it'll be just like in the book when Ronald kidnapped you on that fateful night and you were wearing them, along with your under shorts of course."

At the sound of the "new Ronald" addressing him as "Laddy" a shiver of true trepidation crawled up the ticklish guy's spine.

"Okay Ronald, uh, how about taking those pictures and I'll be on my way, yes?" Timmy asked, sounding nervous as all hell.

He realized as Ronald snapped a few pictures of him what a mistake this had been. He had not told Christopher or Vince where he was headed when he left the hotel earlier than expected. He had not told Stephanie that he would be making a quick stop before heading to the airport. The store that the "new Ronald" owned was closed...and no one, NO ONE, knew he had ventured into this tickle trap. Well, so far it was only his own conclusion that he had walked into a tickle trap. The "new Ronald" had only fastened him to the "Spinning Chinaman" for picture authenticity, he hoped, *he prayed.*

"Oh man Timmy my laddy, these pictures will be awesome when it comes to selling the "Christopher Trevor" books, wouldn't you agree?" the "new Ronald" chuckled as he zoomed in for some close-up shots of Timmy.

"Uh, sure, uh, when all are you going to let me off this thing Ronald?" Timmy asked and his cock pounded fear hard in his kangaroo pouch style under shorts.

A few times the "new Ronald" snapped pictures of the tent in Timmy's under shorts. A few times he snapped pictures of Timmy's socked and bound feet.

"Well, I still have to get some shots of you rotating in that thing and then maybe even take a video of you spinning round and round in there...what do you think buddy?" the "new Ronald" asked and snapped a few pictures of Timmy's face as the twisted reality of this sank in.

"Oh my word," was Timmy's reply.

He knew then that what he had surmised was correct...he had been tricked yet again and this time he had walked into his own ticklish demise. It was slowly dawning on him that his plan had gone awry. This would not be an experience just for him. This would prove to be yet another ticklish experience and he would be serving yet another's twisted jolly needs... As his cock pounded harder in his under shorts he felt his balls shifting around involuntarily in their sexy sweaty sac. It was the same feeling he had gotten when Christopher had Viagra induced him over the weekend.

"Oh jeez, you slipped me a Mickey of some sort in that coffee Ronald," Timmy said as the guy again snapped pictures of his stiffening tented underpants.

"Sure did my laddy, and guess what? There's plenty more where that came from," the "new Ronald" said jovially. "I plan to keep you stacked up and erect for the duration. Ever experienced edging my laddy?"

"Edging, oh my word, that's when a poor guy is all worked up in the cock and he can't get the relief he craves," Timmy replied. "Christopher did the reverse of that to me during our time together this past weekend..."

"Lucky you, and him too," the "new Ronald" chuckled meanly. "But again, for while you're here I'm going to edge you till you're mad with it..."

"And just how long do you plan on keeping me pray tell?" Timmy asked through clenched teeth, it no longer a secret that he had been captured yet again for some ticklish devilry.

"Well, lets see, I'll want at least three rolls of film like this of you, then maybe a good couple of hours of video of you spinning in that thing. But not to worry Laddy I won't spin you for long intervals. I'll videotape you spinning for fifteen to twenty minute sessions until it all adds up to a couple of hours on video. I think that's reasonable, and of course the customers will get a charge out of seeing a model in the "Spinning Chinaman"," the "new Ronald" stated matter of factly as Timmy's jaw dropped.

"So I would think we're looking at, hmm, at least three days my laddy," the "new Ronald" said and smiled behind his camera and snapped off a few pictures of Timmy's look of horror as tears welled in the laddy's eyes.

"OHHHHH, oh my word!" Timmy was bantering a few scant moments later after the "new Ronald" had taken the pin out of the "Spinning Chinaman" that held it fast and the ticklish guy now found himself spinning round and round in a clockwise direction.

And to Timmy's horror the "new Ronald" did not need to spin the device manually, rather he had an electronic hand-held remote control that controlled the rotation of the Chinaman.

With his fingers clenched into fists and his toes curled back under his black socks Timmy spun round and round in the Chinaman as the "new Ronald" snapped picture after picture.

"OH MY WORD of words let me off this thing Ronald!" Timmy cried out miserably. "You all can't keep me here for three days man! I have a flight to catch in a couple of hours..."

"Sorry to burst your bubble Laddy, but that flight has been canceled," the "new Ronald" said and snapped a few pictures of Timmy as he spun upside down and then right side up again, round and round he went. "I'm sure your airline will re-schedule you though...once you're out of here that is..."

As the "new Ronald" chuckled he put his camera down on the shelf and a few moments later he was videotaping Timmy as he spun in the Chinaman.

"I-I'm startin' to feel a tad disoriented in here Ronald," Timmy complained, his strapped hands clenched into fists as he rotated round and round.

"Another of my specialty coffees will fix you right up Timmy my laddy," the "new Ronald" laughed meanly behind his video camera as he recorded the poor Southern guy's plight.

"Oh my, how do I always wind up in these danged predicaments?" Timmy chided himself.

After a good fifteen minutes of videotaping the spinning Timmy Ronald turned off the video camera, stopped Timmy rotating and set the guy in the Chinaman at an upright position, locking the pin in to keep it stabilized. Timmy did not even bother to ask again to be released as he knew it was pointless. He was the tickle hero of many a tickler and the "new Ronald" was his latest vanquisher. MY WORD!

"OOOOOOOOO HAHAHAHAHAHAHAHA!" Timmy was laughing and screaming a few scant seconds later as the "new Ronald" stroked his stomach area with a sharp-tipped goose feather.

Timmy squirmed miserably in the Chinaman and did a sexy sort of dance in his bondage as the "new Ronald" trailed the feather tip over his stomach region, his ribs, his pectorals and it was when he teased Timmy's nipples with the feather that Timmy really howled his song of laughter...

"Oh my word my laddy, oh my word," the "new Ronald" chuckled, sounding real sinister and imitating Timmy's Southern accent not all that well.

Timmy laughed louder and more and more uncontrollably as the "new Ronald" trailed the feather tip over his entire stomach area, upwards over his muscular chest and back down again and again in a circular-like motion...

The "new Ronald" then, about a half hour later had brazenly taken Timmy's erect cock and his sweaty balls out of the fly opening of his kangaroo pouch style underpants. Timmy bantered and swore like a marine at this latest invasion of his manhood, telling the "new Ronald" not to be helping himself to the good stuff between his legs. But Timmy's erection stuck out like a flag pole and his juicy balls dangled like low hangers and swung back and forth a bit as he squirmed and danced bonded in the "Chinaman"...as Ronald tantalized and tease-tickled his piss slit and the shaft of his towering cock with the tip of the goose feather.

"PWWWAHHHHHHHH HAHAHAHAHAHAHA!" Timmy screeched. "OH DANG IT ALL, not my cock Ronald, oh man, not my cock, oh my! HAHAHAHAHAHAHAHAHA!"

To add to Timmy's misery the "new Ronald" had tied Timmy's necktie as a blindfold over Timmy's eyes, thus forcing the poor ticklish guy to really concentrate on and enjoy his latest ticklish trials...

"OH MY WORD, HAHAHAHAHAHAHA!" Timmy catcalled as the "new Ronald" slid the tip of the feather into his piss hole and spun it, tickling the walls of Timmy's inner cock head.

The way Timmy's cock was stiff and sticking straight out made it all so easy for the "new Ronald" to penetrate the sexy piss hole with the tip of his feather. Beads of piss and oozing pre cum emanated from Timmy's cock hole.

"Looks like you have a bit of a problem in the area of your cock bud," the "new Ronald" teased Timmy. "Looks like someone needs to uh, cum..."

"You bet your danged bookstore and Christopher Trevor display someone needs to cum, *I got to cum...*" Timmy cried out in between laughing and laughing.

"All in time my laddy, all in good time," the "new Ronald" said and trailed the feather downward and then around and around and over and over Timmy's succulent balls. "We have three days ahead of us and tonight to get to all the good stuff Timmy... I do plan to milk you dry, I plan to play with those balls of yours...and of course I plan to have at those black socked feet of yours in pure tickle fashion... but for the next couple of days I'm going to keep you balanced on the edging edge, or to be more precise, balanced in the Chinaman..."

Scant seconds later "the new Ronald" had Timmy turned upside down in the "Spinning Chinaman." In blindfolded darkness Timmy looked upwards and laughed like a hyena as the "new Ronald" now tickled the bottoms of his upturned black socked feet, his fingertips strumming them together at the same time...

"YAAAAAHHHHHHHH HAHAHAHAHAHAHA! Ronald, PL-please stop, oh PLEASE STOP!" Timmy cried out laughingly and as he called out the name "Ronald" he recalled with woe once before, or many times before calling out that very name during his awful ticklish trials.

As his feet were tickled Timmy laughed and screamed...

His erect cock stuck straight out and his sweaty balls pressed against it as he lay in the upside down position, feeling beyond disoriented at that point... Droplets of piss and pre cum dripped onto his lips as he laughed and laughed...

Then, Timmy was back upright in the "Spinning Chinaman" as once more the "new Ronald" forced his blindfolded captive to sip down a second coffee, this one doubly laced with his potent aphrodisiac...

Timmy made gluggling sounds as he swallowed the brew, the "new Ronald" holding the laddy's nose tight as he guzzled.

"There you go Timmy my laddy, down the hatch buddy," the "new Ronald" teased and Timmy grimaced when the guy pecked him on the cheek.

He somehow wished he had spent the remaining time with Christopher and Vince at the hotel, at least that way he would not be trapped and tethered to a replica of Valerie's torturous device...he would no doubt be being tickle tortured in some fashion but no way would he have been a "Real" kidnap victim...

When he was done drinking the coffee Timmy breathed heavily and gasped "Oh my" as his cock twitched big and long in front of him. When the "new Ronald" packed him back into his underpants along with his thickly filled balls Timmy again gasped at the guy's touch. He also felt a sense of woe as the guy was not going to give him a man's relief, a relief he desperately craved at that moment. OH DANG, where was Christopher to milk him when he really needed it?

Having been tickled and sexed up with yet another potent aphrodisiac Timmy was feeling very perilously balanced on the edge...

A few moments later the "new Ronald" wiped Timmy's lips clean of the coffee remnants and Timmy pouted as duct tape was wound round and round his mouth and neck, effectively gagging him...

"MMMFFFFF..." Timmy sputtered as the "new Ronald" said, "What a catch, Timmy Backman himself strapped into the "Spinning Chinaman" in my Christopher Trevor bookstore display..."

Timmy made another angry sounding "MMMFFF" sound as the duct tape was sheared at the back of his neck and was now stuck tightly to his lips.

"Yes, Timmy Backman in the flesh and in the socks and kangaroo pouch under shorts too...I'm sure that I'll sell a million dollars worth of books over the next few days..." the "new Ronald" said happily.

Then, with a black spandex hood over his head Timmy nearly cried miserably as the "Spinning Chinaman" slowly spun, as Ronald closed and locked the display room of his favorite author...leaving Timmy alone for the time being...

Timmy's Sensitive Man Nips
(The Day after The Fundraiser)

"AAAAWWWHHHH GAWD, hate to say it, but that feels awesome Sir Leekalot," Timmy Backman, ticklish hero, grunted as he lay half sprawled on his desk in his office at work with his socked feet dangling off the side of said desk.

"Just relax and go with flow as they say Mr. Bockman," the muscular Japanese man who had taken Timmy's desk chair said as he sat and tweaked, squeezed and twisted Timmy's fleshy, luscious, and ultra-sensitive man tits.

"Th-that's Backman with an A, not Bockman with an O, Sir Leekalot," Timmy said breathlessly, grinning stupidly as he lay propped up on his elbows on his own desk as this man made sport with his nipples. "AAAAAAHHHHHHH fucking fucks...oh double fucking fucks *indeed* Sir Leekalot..."

"Yes, yes, with an A," the Japanese man said and smiled down almost lovingly at Timmy as Timmy arched his head back and looked upward at the man who had so beguiled him and literally taken over his office at the bank. "Now face forward or else blindfold goes on you Mr. Bockman..."

"Sure, sure thing Sir Leekalot, but again, that's Backman with an A, not Bockman with an O," Timmy panted and faced forward. "Wouldn't want to be blindfolded for all this fun and enjoyment now either..."

The handsome Japanese man smiled and nuzzled his nose against the side of Timmy's neck as he went on and on tweaking, twisting and squeezing the handsome executive's nipples. Timmy chuckled a bit as the Japanese man's nose tickled his neck ever so slightly...

"HHHHHOOOOOOO, fucking sensations are unreal Sir Leekalot," Timmy said and glanced over at his suit pants, his white button down shirt, his suit jacket and tie as they lay strewn on an office chair.

Timmy's wingtips were on the floor under the chair and as the Japanese man played twist, squeeze and tease with his nipples Timmy glanced nervously at his office door.

"I-I really hope no one happens to come in here Sir Leekalot," Timmy said and almost made the mistake of arching his head back and looking up at the Japanese man. "I-I would hate to be caught this way, with my pants down, I mean *off*, so to speak..."

Again Timmy smiled stupidly, glanced down at the man's magical hands and fingers as they worked his nipples and he curled his toes back under his black nylon office socks... Timmy could recall very vividly how over the time of his life his nipples had always been as sensitive as his cock, as sensitive as a woman's nipples, maybe even more sensitive than a woman's. All someone had to do was mention Timmy's thick-skinned and beefy nipples and he was putty in their hands...so to speak.

"Not to worry Mr. Bockman, everyone is out to lunch at this time, as you say," the Japanese man said and gripped Timmy's nipples tighter yet, getting a good loud sounding swoon out of the ticklish laddy. "No chance of anyone interrupting us...ha, ha. Besides all that everyone knows you are in important meeting with me..."

"Y-yeah, so, so true," Timmy breathed heavily, the sensations emanating from his nipples making his cock harder and harder as it stuck out of the fly opening of his white boxer briefs. "But Sir Leekalot, it's Backman with an A, not Bockman with an O."

"As you say with an A," the Japanese man rhymed, laughed and leaned down and this time kissed the side of Timmy's neck.

The sprawled executive on his desk grimaced slightly at that kiss on the neck but the sensations he was feeling overpowered the feelings of liberty that the handsome Japanese businessman had taken with him thus far. Timmy was sprawled halfway on his desk on his back, propped up on his elbows with his socked feet dangling off the end of the desk. He had been stripped down to his white boxer briefs and black nylon calf length socks by this man who had shown up under the pretenses of a meeting concerning the fundraiser the night before and a donation that the man's company wanted to make to the bank in thanks for Timmy's services... Timmy was a bit taken aback at first. Banks don't accept donations. They accept deposits, they accept loan applications, and they accept tax write-offs, but donations? Not on your life bud. But when the Japanese man named Sir Leekalot (where had Timmy heard that name before?) told Timmy and his VP, Jerry Bradshaw that the money he planned to donate to the bank could in turn be donated to the bank's favorite charity Jerry bit, as did Timmy... Jerry told Timmy to take Sir Leekalot back to his office and set up all the necessary paperwork. The charity that Jerry figured the money could be donated to would be the organization that Timmy had wound up at as a human salad, although that much Jerry Bradshaw was in the dark about. All Jerry cared about, as usual, was that this would be good PR for the bank...and for his yearly bonus. Sir Leekalot thanked the ruggedly good-looking Jerry Bradshaw, shook hands with him and then with Timmy's arm in a firm grasp he walked with the laddy back to Timmy's office. As Timmy strode down the corridor from Jerry's office to his he could not help recalling the Japanese man at Bull's fundraiser the night before. The man had expressed an intense interest in tickling Timmy's big nipples as he lay tied to a salad table, he himself being the main ingredient in that salad. Gawd almighty, what a night that had turned out to be buds Timmy thought in anguish, captured, stripped of his business suit down to his birthday suit, tied the fuck to a huge salad table and tickle tortured all the live long night by the fundraiser participants. Upon entering Jerry Bradshaw's office and seeing Sir Leekalot sitting opposite Jerry at his desk Timmy had not made mention of the fact that he recognized this man from the fundraiser the night before. More than anything he wanted to see where this was going to go. When it was said that it was going to go toward money for the bank Timmy's greed once more got the best of him... He knew that this transaction, if handled properly could mean a huge bonus for him at the end of the year... Okay, he knew the man from the fundraiser, but his name, Leekalot, Leekalot, where had Timmy heard that danged name? For the life of him he just couldn't seem to place it... All that business of the Japanese businessman making a donation to the bank had transpired first thing in the morning at nine AM. After the early meeting in Jerry's office Timmy took Sir Leekalot directly to his private office...and that was when the tit fun and excitement had begun...and it had not yet stopped, even by lunch time...

And now Timmy Backman, banker and tickle hero was having his man tits (as he called them) mauled and worked over by a handsome Japanese man named Sir Leekalot, who, for whatever the reason could not seem to get Timmy's last name correctly pronounced...

"You enjoy having tits worked this way yes Mr. Bockman?" Sir Leekalot asked his prey.

"Y-yeah, yeah, I suppose I do at that," Timmy replied, the evidence of his enjoyment sticking out of his boxer briefs big and beefy and hard attesting to what he said. "But like I said, its' Backman with an A, not Bockman with an O."

Timmy arched his crotch area upward and his hard cock swung in the wind as his juicy balls throbbed and churned, chock-filled with the ticklish laddy's thick spunk. He groaned in a man's passion...

"Yes, yes, with an A again," the Japanese man said almost seductively as Timmy's head leaned back further and rested momentarily on Sir Leekalot's shoulder. "Oh yes Mr. Bockman, you are enjoy this very much, ha, ha..."

"Yeah, very much," Timmy panted, propped himself a tad higher on his elbows, clenched his hands into tight fists, and again recalled how the man had leaned over him at the fundraiser as he lay tied to the salad table, sweating and smelling of oil and vinegar.

The Japanese man hadn't seemed all that interested in tickling poor Timmy, although for the purposes of the fundraiser he had tickled him; tickled his man tits to be precise...tickled poor Timmy's man tits with swizzle sticks that had been provided by Bull and his blasted cohorts. When Timmy had been wheeled to Sir Leekalot's table the Japanese businessman seemed instantly and at once mesmerized by the ticklish laddy's jutted up and hard nipples. After all the tickling Timmy had already endured his man tits really were pointing north. God knew that when Timmy was relentlessly tickled it caused his man tits (and other parts of him) to really coagulate and harden. Timmy had laughed his head off at the tingly and ticklish sensations as they emanated from his man tits to his cock... All his life Timmy had said that his sensitive man tits were indeed hotwired to his big beefy cock...

And now, the next day Timmy found himself in his office at the bank, of all places, laying half on and half off his desk, stripped and being used as the Japanese man's tit play machine... Leekalot...Leekalot... Where oh where had Timmy heard that name before he asked himself...

Timmy glanced over at a picture of his wife Stephanie that he kept on his desk and said to himself, "Oh babe, if you could see your handsome hubby now. Oh the things I do for this company I work for..."

"Most men do not know how wonderful it can feel to have tits compressed and squashed like this yes Mr. Bockman with an A?" the Japanese man asked Timmy teasingly as he did just that, mashed the laddy's nipples in his thumbs and fingers.

"Uh yeah, I mean, no, they don't know how gr-great it can feel," Timmy replied and propped himself up still a tad higher on his elbows. "And it's Backman with an A, not Bockman with an A, er, an O, oh what the fucking fucks...OHHHHRRRRRRR..."

The Japanese man chuckled and then took Timmy's nipples by the very tips of them. He giggled as he twirled his fingers in a clockwise and then a counter clockwise direction, really sending spinning spirals through the laddy's brain...and his cock...

"Round and round your man tits go yes Mr. Backman without an O?" the Japanese man chuckled.

"Al-although a lot of guys out there are learning that their tits, *their man tits* are a real erogenous zone Sir Leekalot..." Timmy said and seethed as his nipples were whirled.

"Yes, man tits Mr. Bockman, very good way of calling tits," Leekalot snuffed and kissed Timmy's neck again.

"It, its Backman with an A," Timmy whispered. "Gawd, but my man tits are sensitive as all hell...And, and Gawd, like you said, round and round they go, with what you're doin' with 'em they really are bein' spun good and hefty like I must say..."

"What makes man tits more sensitive and susceptible is after man whose tits are played with shoots load," Leekalot said, making Timmy's hard cock twitch with a life all its own at the sound of those words. "After a man shoots a load or two or three, ha, ha, his man's tits are even more highly sensitive..."

"T-two or three loads Sir Leekalot?" Timmy sputtered. "Wh-what in all tarnation are you plannin' on here?"

Without another word the Japanese man let go of Timmy's nipples, pushed Timmy forward to a seated position atop his desk, grabbed Timmy's shoulders and turned him around atop the desk facing him... Timmy spun easily on his cotton briefs atop the desk... Being spun around on his briefs atop his desk like a top Timmy thought of the scene in the movie "Risky Business" where Tom Cruise made his dancing entrance sliding on a wood floor in white sweat socks...

"OH, OH GAWD," Timmy blubbered and stretched his arms out and pressed his fingers against his desktop as the Japanese man's head dove down and his mouth devoured Timmy's hard cock.

He sucked Timmy's cock and Timmy's head spun, almost resembling Linda Blair's head in the Exorcist and his tits churned all numb and tingly...

"FUCKING fucks, say Sir Leekalot, what kind of a donation are we talking here?" Timmy panted and huffed, his head thrown back as his cock was serviced expertly. "Just what kind of a number are we looking at? I mean, okay, my, my danged man tits are one thing, but now you got my manhood in your mouth here and you know, I got me a wife..."

As Timmy spoke and huffed he looked down at the Japanese man between his legs.

"My word..." Timmy muttered softly. "F-feels like some kind of suction device has been hooked up to manhood..."

Sir Leekalot slid his velvety feeling tongue along the shaft and the thick veins of Timmy's huge erection as he held it captive in his mouth. His lips worked some kind of erotic magic all around the crown-tip of the laddy's manhood. Timmy swooned as the man caressed his socked calves and sucked him harder and deeper... Sir Leekalot's tongue tip trailed the outlines of the veins on Timmy's cock as he momentarily held the beef stick in hand and then slurped it heartily back into his craw, sending stormy chills through the black socked executive...

"H-how much?" Timmy panted and sweated as the man lapped his balls and again slurped his cock quickly back into his mouth. "FUCKING totally fucks, for what I'm enduring here I figure on a big fat figure Sir

Leekalot...I'm a married guy after all..."

The Japanese man stopped sucking Timmy for a moment, looked up at him and smiled a triumphant smile.

"Not to worry Mr. Bockman, your vice president Jerry Bradshaw will be most happy with the figure I plan to offer..." Sir Leekalot said and leaned back down to retrieve Timmy's cock in his mouth.

"AAAWWWW, I s-sure hope so Sir Leekalot," Timmy grunted breathlessly, looking down as the man's cheeks seemed to inflate as he serviced Timmy's cock. "L-Leekalot, wh-where the fucking fuck have I heard that name before?"

Smiling wickedly Sir Leekalot took Timmy's cock again from his mouth and grasped the ticklish laddy by the root of his balls, tugging them downward really hard... Timmy nearly flew off the desk as the Japanese man trailed a fingertip over the tip of Timmy's pre seed oozing erection. Chills and thrills coursed through Timmy's muscular body.

"Yes, where indeed have you heard Leekalot Mr. Bockman with no O?" Sir Leekalot teased the ticklish hero and again leaned down to gulp Timmy's erection greedily into his mouth.

Every time the man slurped Timmy's erection into his mouth Timmy nearly flew off his desk... A short while later Timmy spewed a huge load of man juice and the greedy Japanese businessman swallowed it with gusto... Like an explosion happening between his muscular legs Timmy shot a load big enough to choke a horse...

"OHHHHHRRRRR ooooooooo," Timmy swooned atop his desk as he fed his creamy hot load to the Japanese man named Sir Leekalot.

As Timmy came he curled his toes back under his socks and he again tried to recall just where exactly he had heard the name Leekalot in the past... But at the moment his thoughts were all fuzzy as his balls gave up their juices and his muscle pipe spewed its load down the Japanese businessman's esophagus...

"Oh yes, oh fucking fucks yes Sir Leekalot," Timmy grunted and huffed real throatily.

He pressed his palms hard against his desk, curled his toes back under his socks and clenched his teeth as he thrust his crotch area slightly up and down on his desk, his manhood plunged way down deep in the Japanese man's throat. Timmy was spurred on more-so by the sounds of swallowing as Sir Leekalot downed his creamy load...

When Timmy was done spewing his juices the Japanese man wasted no time. He quickly spun Timmy back on his desk, facing away from him, reached around him and again grabbed Timmy's nipples in his thumbs and fingers.

"AAAAAAHHHRRRRRHHH..." Timmy bantered.

"What I said is true yes Mr. Bockman?" Leekalot asked Timmy. "Man tits are now even more sensitive, yes, yes?"

"HUHHHHH! Y-yes Sir, man tits are A LOT more sensitive now!" Timmy seethed. "OHHHHH, my word, MY FUCKING FUCKS!"

"By way Mr. Bockman, you taste what you Americans call magnificent..." the Japanese man said and smacked his lips together contentedly. "Real nice egg-roll you are sporting there between sexy legs. I am sure you must make wife very happy..."

"Jeez, thanks for the compliment Sir Leekalot, but again, it's..." Timmy began.

"Yes, with an A," Sir Leekalot laughed and stretched the flesh of Timmy's nipples forward, really squeezing them now.

"OOOWWWWW!" Timmy bellowed. "I really hope all this will be worth my trouble when you write that check for the bank Sir Leekalot..."

"It will be well worth it Mr. Bockman, very well worth it," the Japanese man said and kissed Timmy's earlobe.

Timmy glanced down again and saw that the Japanese businessman was really stretching his man tits forward, obviously trying to find out just how much elasticity was in them. When Timmy cried out in erotic pain the Japanese man chuckled and took Timmy's man tits next by the sides, really grabbing at the beef of them... He gyrated his fingers up and down against the sides of Timmy's nipples really sending chills through the ticklish young man now...

"OHHHHHRRRRR fuck..." Timmy sighed.

"I can play with man tits all day Mr. Bockman..." Sir Leekalot whispered in Timmy's ear and gave his earlobe a nip with his front-most teeth.

"For fuck's sake, it's Backman..." Timmy panted through clenched teeth and looked down at his black socked feet. "Gawd, you got me sweatin' in my socks here..."

As the laddy looked down at his black socked feet he, for whatever the fuck the reason thought of his villainous buddy Ronald...his cock twitched and began to stiffen yet again...

"I will drink from you again Mr. Bockman with an A," Sir Leekalot teased Timmy as he squeezed the sides of Timmy's beefed up man tits.

By now Timmy's nipples were harder than pebbles and erect beyond any other time that he could recall in his life...

Sir Leekalot spun his fingers back and forth, spinning Timmy's man tits, making Timmy's head spin... Gawd almighty, but this man really knew how to use the magic touch when it came to Timmy's nipples the ticklish laddy thought in a fuzzy haze...

"Leekalot, ohhhhhhrrrrr for the fucking fuck second time that's what I'm doin' here Sir Leekalot," Timmy panted with a smile on his face. "I'm sure leaking a lot..."

"Will do something about that very soon Mr. Bockman..." Sir Leekalot laughed along with the sexed up Timmy.

"OHHHHRRRR GAWD, y-you're takin' control of my cock here Sir Leekalot..." Timmy panted and arched his crotch upwards.

After a good fifteen to twenty minutes more of continuous and non-stop tit play Sir Leekalot spun Timmy around once more on his desk facing him. He trailed his palms up and down Timmy's socked calves and took in the sight of Timmy's cum and saliva sticky erection...

"You ready to, as you Americans say, blow load number two for me Mr. Bockman with an A?" the Japanese man asked Timmy.

"Y-yeah, whatever the fuck you say Sir Leekalot, you're the one donating the money, I'm just a working stiff here huh?" Timmy asked sarcastically in reply.

"Hang on tight then, as you American's say Mr. Bockman," Sir Leekalot chuckled and lowered his head down to Timmy's crotch. "It is again time for takeoff, ha, ha..."

"AWWWWWWW and here we go again..." Timmy panted as his office guest sucked him heartily and with true blue gusto.

Sir Leekalot held tight to Timmy's balls as his head bobbed up and down on Timmy's erect cock... Timmy swooned and sat back on the palms of his hands as he was sucked toward gusher number two... The Japanese businessman held Timmy's family jewels tighter as he feasted on Timmy's thick veined and throbbing flagpole of a cock...

"Wh-what a day this turned out to be eh Sir Leekalot?" Timmy asked stupidly.

"Mmmm..." was all the Japanese businessman said while his mouth was full.

He tugged Timmy's balls and the laddy found himself leaning back further on the palms of his hands atop his desk.

"AAAAAAHHHHHHH..." Timmy swooned and his office seemed to spin in front of him.

This man who had tickled him mercilessly the night before at the fundraiser was now making amends it seemed...

Timmy's briefs covered bottom bobbed up and down on his desk as he fed Sir Leekalot his cock from the fly opening of said briefs.

"OOOOOOO yeah, fucking A!" Timmy seethed and bobbed faster on his desk.

A few minutes later Sir Leekalot was again chowing down on Timmy's leaking cock as it spewed sexy mess number two...

"AAAAWWWWW GAWD," Timmy nearly shrieked but remembered that he was at work and did not want anyone who happened to be passing by his office to hear him in the throes of ecstasy.

"MMMMM, HMMMM," Sir Leekalot murmured as he swallowed Timmy's globs and globs of protein.

When Timmy was done Sir Leekalot stood up to stretch his legs, Timmy sitting docilely in front of him on his desk. It truly astounded Timmy how his office guest was still properly dressed in his business attire while he, the office host as he would be called in these circumstances, was clad in no more than his boxer briefs and office socks.

"As you American's say Mr. Bockman, feeling good?" Sir Leekalot asked Timmy and tousled the laddy's hair.

"Y-yeah, as we say, I'm feelin' real good Sir Leekalot..." Timmy replied as the Japanese man tweaked his nipples from the front this time.

"How man tits feel now Mr. Bockman with an A?" Sir Leekalot asked, sounding totally mischievous.

"OOOOOOOO, af-after shooting two loads they're excessively sensitive now I would have to say..." Timmy panted.

"Ha, ha, good assessment Mr. Bockman, you keep up this good

work you are doing and donation will be higher yet..." Sir Leekalot teased Timmy and with brute strength spun Timmy back on his desk facing away from him.

"UHHHHFFFF!" Timmy grunted as he spun on his desk.

Looking down Timmy watched as the man's hands snaked again toward his erect nipples...

"FUCKING FUCKS Sir Leekalot, you sure do love my man tits..." Timmy drawled as Sir Leekalot grabbed his man tits yet again.

"You keep face forward or else..." the Japanese man began.

"I know, I know, blindfold goes on..." Timmy finished the sentence for him. "OHHHHRRRR GAWD, but you were right Sir! After a guy cums his man tits sure as shit are overly sensitized! I'm feeling like a thousand fingers are working my man tits right about now!"

"All good Mr. Bockman with the A," Sir Leekalot laughed. "My fingers have been called magic over years by both women and some men, you being one of the men, ha, ha. And as you Americans also say, third time is the charm, yes?"

"Wh-whatever you say Sir Leekalot, wh-whatever the fucking fuck you say..." Timmy hemmed breathlessly.

"Oh, so witty, so funny how you Americans use swear words when you are in what you call the throes of ecstasy..." the Japanese man teased Timmy and kissed his neck. "Tell me Mr. Bockman with no O but an A, does your wife tease your man tits this way?"

"Sh-she teases me in other ways, OHHHRRRR FUCK," Timmy seethed as Leekalot again took his man tits right by the very tips of them. "Seems like that's when they're most sensitive Sir Leekalot, when you grate the tips of my danged nubs..."

"Then we will go for more as you Americans say..." Sir Leekalot whispered in Timmy's ear.

As Timmy's nipples were being worked like crazy he stretched his long legs out in front of him as they dangled off the end of his desk... Again, looking at his black socked feet he, for whatever the fuck the reason thought of Ronald. Ronald, who once again had been there after the tickle festivities were over. Ronald had been at the fundraiser the night before. And lo and fucking behold why wouldn't he have not been there? It was a tickle-fest after all and everyone knows by now how much Ronald loves tickling. Or, to be more precise, everyone knows by now how much Ronald loves tickling his good buddy Timmy. And once again like with other times when Timmy had found himself in tickle trouble Ronald had offered to drive the handsome laddy home, once he had been un-saladed of course and cleaned himself up. But once again, instead of being driven directly home to Stephanie and his son the poor laddy found himself enroute for another trite of tickle fun at Ronald's tickle palace, a place safely hidden away somewhere in upper New York City. Ronald had had the chloroform at the ready as usual. Would Timmy ever learn he asked himself for what seemed like the umpteenth time? When Timmy had come to he told Ronald what a shitty thing it was to do to a poor guy to hang him upside down by his ankles, naked as the day he was born while a mechanical device fastened to the ceiling tickled the bottoms of your feet...

Now Timmy knew why he thought of Ronald every time he looked at his black socked feet. The black socks were his so called buddies' favorites... Timmy thought in a silly way how he would never wear black socks again, but that was of course an impossibility, seeing as he was a banker after all...GAWD!

"AAAAHHHHH..." Timmy moaned as his mind returned to the present as Sir Leekalot tweaked the tips of his nipples.

"I will have another drink from you soon Mr. Bockman, like we said before, third time will be the charm," Sir Leekalot chuckled.

"Y-yeah, it sure as all fucks will be Sir Leekalot," Timmy panted and his mind drifted and whirled to that morning when he had been summoned to Jerry Bradshaw's office.

It had started out as a day like any other. Timmy arrived at work promptly at eight fifty five AM, ready to start the workday at nine. The handsome laddy, clad in a fresh gray suit, white shirt, gray and black silk necktie and black wingtips was still feeling a bit tired and tingly from the previous night's adventures. Timmy chuckled under his breath as he stepped off the elevator and thought how not all bankers who attend a fundraiser wind up being a human salad and tickle tortured all the live long night. And then spirited off to a tickle palace, lets not forget that buds. By the time Ronald *had* brought him home Timmy was so exhausted that he fell promptly into bed beside Stephanie with his socks and underpants still on. Amazing that he had risen and shined for work on time the next morning

Timmy thought as he walked down the corridor toward his office, a brown bag containing a cup of coffee and a bagel in hand. He was at his desk and enjoying the hot coffee when his in-office phone rang.

"Backman," Timmy said into the receiver.

Timmy listened as Jerry Bradshaw's secretary told him that he was wanted in the vice president's office right away.

"Starting my day off right away eh?" Timmy asked in a humorous sounding tone. "Probably he wants to hear all about the fundraiser."

Timmy thanked the secretary, told her he would be there in a moment and hung up the phone. As he walked the short distance to Jerry's office Timmy simply figured that he would skip the part at the fundraiser where Frank Brucco, AKA Bull the bartender had had him stripped, tied up and turned into the centerpiece of a huge salad. Timmy figured he would just tell Jerry about the final figure that had been agreed upon by himself and Mr. Brucco. When Timmy got to Jerry's office he, as always, politely knuckle knocked twice. He heard Jerry's booming voice call out; "Come on in Timmy!" Timmy entered the office and nearly jumped out of his shoes and socks when he saw Sir Leekalot seated opposite the vice president's desk...

"Good morning there Timmy, had a good time last night at the fundraiser?" Jerry asked in greeting as with a trembling hand Timmy closed the office door.

"Uh, yes Sir, a very good time," Timmy replied, sounding a tad unsure as he stepped over to the vice president's desk and shook Jerry's outstretched hand.

"That's what Sir Leekalot here was telling me just now," Jerry said. "I'm sure you remember him from the event last night. He's been telling me how you and he discussed some future business for the bank...this morning being the future to be exact Backman."

"Uh yes, we uh, we discussed stuff last night, that, that's for sure," Timmy said as Jerry released his hand and the handsome Japanese businessman quickly got to his feet.

"Timmy, you of course remember Sir Leekalot," Jerry said as the man bowed and then took Timmy's hand in his almost lovingly and shook it.

"I-I sure do Mr. Bradshaw," Timmy stuttered, addressing Jerry by his last name for the purposes of the impromptu meeting he had been shanghaied into.

"Mr. Bockman was very receptive to me at fundraiser last night," Sir Leekalot said with an evil looking smile as he seemed to drink in the sight of the laddy as Timmy's eyes almost betrayed his fear, the fear being that Jerry would find out that he had spent the previous evening naked, tied up and tickle tortured.

"Well, let's all sit down and discuss this shall we?" Jerry asked. "Although Timmy, Sir Leekalot here and you will make the final arrangements and you'll handle all the paperwork."

"In your office Mr. Bockman..." Sir Leekalot said as they all sat down, Jerry behind his desk and Sir Leekalot and Timmy opposite him in office chairs.

"Yes, sure thing, in my office," Timmy said and nervously tugged his tie.

As Timmy looked at Sir Leekalot his nipples tingled as he recalled the Japanese businessman swirling those danged swizzle sticks all over and around them...really tickling them and making him cackle like a hyena.

"Okay Timmy, Sir Leekalot represents a huge Japanese novelty company," Jerry said, leaning forward with his elbows on his desk. "What he's proposing is a donation to the bank...for the services we *and you* rendered last night at the fundraiser..."

"A, a donation to the bank?" Timmy asked and nearly flew out of his chair as Sir Leekalot crossed one leg and pressed the tip of a shiny cap-toe against the laddy's calf, unseen by Jerry of course. "But uh, Mr. Bradshaw, Sir, the bank doesn't accept donations..."

"Good point and Sir Leekalot knows that," Jerry said.

Timmy was sweating in his socks as the Japanese businessman trailed the tip of his cap toe upwards against Timmy's leg. Glancing down, Timmy saw that Sir Leekalot was wearing very sheer black socks with his cap toe shoes. At the sight of those sheer, sheer socks Timmy fleetingly thought of Valerie and how at times she favored sheer stockings. His cock started to spout a stiffy in his suit pants, and first thing in the morning at that...hardy har and har...

"So, with that in mind," Jerry went on. "What Sir Leekalot has proposed is that the bank can accept his offer and in turn donate the money to *our* favorite charity..."

"It would make good business for the bank from my company and others when they hear about it Mr. Bockman..." Sir Leekalot said softly, leaning in closer to Timmy as he spoke and then looked over at Jerry Bradshaw.

"So what do you say Timmy?" Jerry asked. "You ready to start your day by getting this off the ground for us?"

Jerry had phrased it as a question but Timmy knew a direct order when he heard one...

Timmy felt Sir Leekalot's shoe press even higher on his calf... So, tugging at his tie Timmy stuttered, "Sure, sure thing Jerry, Mr. Bradshaw..."

"Good deal," Jerry said, getting to his feet, a wide smile on his ruggedly handsome face.

As Jerry stood up so did Sir Leekalot and Timmy... Timmy was glad that his cock had not reached full mast from the teasing that Sir Leekalot had just done to him...but oh Gawd, those sheer socks that the Japanese businessman had on, GAWD! Timmy had to wonder where this so called venture was heading... After what the man had done to him the night before Timmy really had to wonder...

"Sir Leekalot, Timmy will take you to his office where you and he can discuss the final figure you'd like to donate..." Jerry said, shaking hands with the Japanese businessman.

"As you Americans say, sounds good to me..." Sir Leekalot said. "I want to thank you Mr. Bradshaw. You have good man in Mr. Bockman here... When he and me met last night I knew that it was he who I would want...to handle this venture of course..."

"Sure thing then," Jerry drawled, obviously anxious to find out what the figure would be after Sir Leekalot and his boy wonder were done with the upcoming business.

Smiling, Sir Leekalot picked up the half empty coffee cup that he had had on Jerry's desk. He swirled the swizzle stick in it and smiled knowingly at Timmy as he sipped down the last of the brew. Timmy again tugged nervously at his tie... Swizzle sticks, Gawd, the instruments of his torture at Sir Leekalot's hands the night before...

A few moments later Sir Leekalot and Timmy were walking slowly down the corridor toward Timmy's private office, Sir Leekalot holding Timmy's upper arm in a tight grasp...

"He is very nice your vice president Bradshaw," Sir Leekalot said jovially and Timmy's skin crawled and his cock churned as the Japanese businessman held tight to his upper arm.

"What are you really doing here Sir Leekalot?" Timmy fumed softly, not wanting his anger to be evident to anyone they passed who was working at their desks or who passed them in the hallway.

"What do you mean Mr. Bockman?" Sir Leekalot asked, sounding mystified. "All was discussed in Mr. Bradshaw's office."

"You know very well what I mean," Timmy replied and with his arm still in the other man's grasp turned to face him head on.

Sir Leekalot smiled and affectionately grasped Timmy's other arm as he faced him, holding Timmy at half arm's length.

"I am here to make a donation..." Leekalot said.

"I mean why you are here after what you did to me last night at the fundraiser?" Timmy whispered angrily. "That was a shitty thing to do to me with those danged swizzle sticks..."

"Yes, yes Mr. Bockman, very ticklish situation you were in last night, ha, ha..." the Japanese man said with a smirk and grasped Timmy's arms tighter. "I assure you no tickling for now...just...other things...other things..."

As the man spoke he looked at Timmy's shirt and tie and licked his lips in the direction of where Timmy's nipples were...

Timmy gulped hard... In that instant as the Japanese man looked at his chest his nipples tingled under his white dress shirt. The laddy recalled with a mixture of ecstasy and trepidation how this Japanese businessman had made sport the night before with his puffed up nipples. Somehow Timmy knew he was now in for more of the same somehow...

"Shall we proceed to your office now Mr. Bockman?" Sir Leekalot asked.

"It's Backman with an A, not Bockman with an O," Timmy stated as the man let go of his arms and they walked on. "Danged shit that a poor guy in my position has to put up with..."

"Yes, with an A," Sir Leekalot said with a grin and quickly snared Timmy's arm back in his claw-like grasp once more as they approached the handsome executive's office.

Once in Timmy's office Sir Leekalot took a moment to really take in the sight of his prey. Timmy stood by his desk feeling totally on display...

"So uh, lets get down to the business at hand here what do you say Sir, uh, Sir Leekalot?" Timmy asked and as he stepped to move behind his desk the handsome and muscular Japanese man blocked his way.

"Don't be in such a hurry Mr. Bockman," Sir Leekalot said, leering mischievously at Timmy. "We have all day, as you Americans say. And your Mr. Bradshaw does want this donation money after all..."

As Leekalot spoke he took Timmy's tie in his fingertips and trailed them up and down the silk black and gray neckwear.

"Okay, then tell me this...just how much of a danged donation is the bank looking at here?" Timmy asked through clenched teeth, doing his staunchest best to hold his ground and try to maintain some semblance of control of the situation.

"Well now, that will depend on you Mr. Bockman, and how well you, how do you Americans say, how well you cooperate..." Sir Leekalot said and tugged Timmy's tie.

"How well I cooperate?" Timmy asked. "What the fucking fucks does that mean? And again, it's Backman with an A."

"Yes, again, with an A," Sir Leekalot said lustfully. "Please, take off suit jacket Mr. Bockman, relax, you are in privacy of your own office after all, yes?"

"T-take off my suit jacket?" Timmy asked in disbelief, but found himself relenting.

Timmy stood docilely as his cock pounded in his suit pants and he allowed the Japanese businessman to help him out of his suit jacket. Sir Leekalot tossed Timmy's expensive suit jacket on an office chair like it was worth nothing.

"Okay then, now we are, as you Americans say, getting down to business," Leekalot purred as he stood behind Timmy and gripped his upper arms tight.

Timmy stared forward and pursed his lips as he was handled...

"Would you like help with your tie too Mr. Bockman?" Sir Leekalot asked and Timmy gulped hard again as the man pressed up against his sexy butt cheeks and with his snake-like fingers took the knot of Timmy's tie in hand.

Timmy could not help but note that the Japanese businessman was sporting a raging hard-on in his suit pants.

"Wh-what the fucking fuck are you doin' to me here Sir Leekalot?" Timmy asked as his tie was slowly undone from behind.

"Just helping you to get more comfy Mr. Bockman, it will help business to flow better. Don't you agree?" Leekalot asked Timmy teasingly.

"Yeah, whatever it takes for the cause eh?" Timmy asked sarcastically as his tie slid off from under his shirt collar. "And it's Backman with an A, not Bockman with an O."

"Yes, yes, no O, but an A," the Japanese man chuckled and what he did next totally astounded the ticklish laddy.

In a fast sweeping motion Sir Leekalot turned Timmy's necktie into a makeshift blindfold by draping it over Timmy's eyes and wrapping the long silk material twice around his head.

"H-hey now, my word, what is this?" Timmy asked, his fingers twitching nervously on both hands as he stood with his hands at his sides. "De-suiting me is one thing here Sir Leekalot, but blindfoldin' me too?"

"It is for good cause Mr. Bockman with an A," Leekalot laughed as he tied a knot in Timmy's tie behind his head. "Not to worry Mr. Bockman, it will help you to relax."

Timmy then felt the Japanese man's fingers undoing his shirt buttons, slowly, one at a time, as he now stood in front of the handsome and blindfolded laddy.

"So tell me Mr. Bockman, how did you wind up as salad last night?" Sir Leekalot asked Timmy meanly as he yanked the laddy's shirt tails from his suit pants.

"I-uh, well, it really wasn't my plan to wind up as a human salad mind you Mr.-er- Sir, *Sir* Leekalot," Timmy drawled nervously as his shirt was taken off him from behind. "But you see, and I can't at the moment, hardy har and har, you see, it was Mr. Brucco, Bull, it was Bull's idea that if I was made into a salad and tickle tortured it would bring in extra money for the tickler organization that he's the head of...you understand I think..."

"Yes, yes, I understand very much Mr. Bockman with the A,"

Sir Leekalot said and un-tucked Timmy's frosty white tee shirt from his suit pants next. "When I saw you tied up to salad table I somehow got feeling that you were not exactly one hundred percent happy with your situation..."

The Japanese man marveled lustfully and longingly as Timmy's jutted up nipples pressed hard and invitingly against his tee shirt.

"Arms up and over head Mr. Bockman," Sir Leekalot ordered and Timmy reluctantly did as he was told.

In a quick move Leekalot had Timmy's tee shirt off him. He deposited Timmy's dress shirt and tee shirt on the office chair along with his suit jacket...

"I understand very much that you are what Mr. Bull called a very, *very* ticklish laddy Mr. Bockman," Sir Leekalot said as he guided Timmy next to his desk and leaned his butt against it, propping him there. "Stand still while I am remove your shoes Mr. Bockman..."

"Say uh, Sir Leekalot, why don't you just uh, call me Timmy huh?" Timmy asked, grinning in a silly way behind his blindfold.

"No, no, I always address business people by last name..." the Japanese man said as he unlaced Timmy's wingtips.

"Dang, I'm bein' stripped here..." Timmy whispered.

As he slid the first then the second shoe off Timmy's feet, balancing the laddy by holding tight to his socked ankle as he did so Sir Leekalot looked upwards and again took in the sight of Timmy's nipples. He could not believe that now those nipples looked even more jutted up than they had just a few moments before when he had gotten Timmy's tee shirt off him... It was very obvious to the Japanese businessman that Tim Backman was not only extremely tickle sensitive but also very tit sensitive as well. As he sniffed the inside of Timmy's shoes he looked up adoringly at his blindfolded and befuddled prey... Timmy Backman was a beautiful, beautiful man Sir Leekalot thought to himself as he sniffed heartily at the insides of the blindfolded laddy's wingtips. The scent emanating from Timmy's shoes was a mixture of sweaty nylon from his dress socks and a leathery musty scent as well from his wingtips... Sir Leekalot knew a few artists, painters and photographers who would more than likely give their right arm to have this handsome and ticklish executive model for them... But at the moment he was the lucky one who had Timothy Backman in his clutches. The Japanese businessman thanked the gods and his ancestors for having gone to the "Tickle Event" the previous night. He also thanked his beautiful partner, Makya Leekalot. Oh yes, when Makya had gotten wind of the "Tickle Event" she knew from her past experience in Valerie's office that Timothy Backman would surely be there, in some ticklish capacity...

"So you agreed to be the tickle event's main attraction yes Mr. Bockman?" Sir Leekalot asked Timmy as he held the laddy's shoes in hand.

"Well, I wouldn't say I exactly agreed to it Sir Leekalot," Timmy explained. "But I will say this...Bull, Mr. Brucco that is, Mr. Brucco and his cohorts were pretty convincing, just like you are being right about now I would have to say..."

"Yes, as I said, I could tell last night that you were not exactly happy with being human salad," Sir Leekalot drawled with a chuckle in his voice. "But you laughed anyway...you laughed a lot..."

"I-I couldn't help it Sir Leekalot," Timmy said. "I was bein' tickled after all..."

Sir Leekalot tossed Timmy's wingtips under the office chair where his clothes had piled up and then stood up straight in front of the handsome executive.

"Now it is time to truly unveil you, yes Mr. Bockman?" Leekalot asked Timmy and began undoing the laddy's belt.

Timmy again gulped hard in total disbelief of how his day had started out...

"Uh, yeah, I suppose if you're goin' to bare me on the top you may as well go for the bottom half as well huh?" Timmy snickered. "And uh, Sir Leekalot, it's Backman with an A..."

"Yes, yes, an A Mr. Bockman," the Japanese man said jovially as he undid the fastener on Timmy's suit pants.

Timmy let out an involuntary "Oooop" sort of sound as his suit pants slid down his legs and pooled around his socked ankles.

"Very sexy you are Mr. Bockman with the A," Sir Leekalot chuckled and balanced Timmy by his upper arms as he stepped one foot at a time out of his suit pants.

The Japanese businessman tossed Timmy's suit pants on the office chair with the rest of his attire and then stood taking in the sight of Mr.

Timmy Backman, whom he just seemed to love calling Mr. Bockman.

"Dang it all, you really stripped me good here Sir Leekalot," Timmy said as he stood propped against his desk, his fingers and thumbs gripping the side of the desk behind him, his cock rage hard and snaking out of the fly opening of his white boxer briefs.

"I will leave underpants and socks on you Mr. Bockman," Sir Leekalot said, taking Timmy by his arms and drawing him a few steps away from his desk.

"Gee, what can I say?" Timmy asked sarcastically as Sir Leekalot stepped behind him. "Thanks for leavin' me with some modesty here..."

"Now we will, as you Americans say, get down to business here, yes Mr. Bockman?" the Japanese man asked Timmy and standing behind him reached slowly around the blindfolded laddy.

Timmy felt the sleeves of Sir Leekalot's suit jacket as his arms trailed against his sides...

"Say, what have you got in mind here Sir Leekalot?" Timmy asked and then received his answer as Sir Leekalot's fingers and thumbs snared his nipples. "UUUULLPP!"

"Last night at fund raiser I tickled your very sexy nips Mr. Bockman, today I will do even more than that to them..." Sir Leekalot whispered in Timmy's ear, nuzzling his nose against the side of Timmy's blindfold.

"OOOOOOOOO, ohhhhhhhhhh Gawd, you really did manage to find two of my most sensitive pleasure points Sir Leekalot..." Timmy huffed as he was drawn a few steps further from his desk, all the while Sir Leekalot was squeezing and twisting his nubs.

"Stand at soldier-like attention Mr. Bockman," Sir Leekalot said commandingly. "If you do all that is told to you I will remove blindfold... eventually..."

"Y-yes Sir," Timmy responded and licked his lips nervously as his nipples were now being played like an accordion as the man who had taken over his office squeezed the bejesus out of them.

"OOOOOOOOOOOO," Timmy hooted.

Timmy swayed on his socked feet, his arms rigidly at his sides as his nipples were accosted... His hard cock jutted out of the fly opening of his boxer briefs, in need of relief...

Timmy stood in that position for nearly a half hour while Sir

Leekalot really whirled and twirled his nipples to a beyond erect and hard state... It was at that point that the Japanese businessman got the handsome laddy situated atop his desk as he continued to play Timmy's nipples like they were a musical instrument. As the morning wore on and Timmy's nipples became numb at moments Sir Leekalot took the blindfold off his prey...

And now, here it was, a few hours later, lunch time to be exact and Timmy was still stripped to his underpants and socks and a virtual tit hostage in his own office. With his sweaty palms pressed hard against the top of his desk Timmy clenched his teeth as Sir Leekalot twisted his oversized and plumped up nipples. Timmy's sore cock was again rage hard, sticking out of his underpants, glistening and sticky with the remnants of Sir Leekalot's saliva and his own seed...

"AAAAAAAHHHHHHHH," Timmy swooned.

"Very soon Mr. Bockman, very soon I will have my final drink from you and then your bank will have very hefty donation..." Sir Leekalot laughed.

"M-my word, I'm feelin' real hefty here right about now Sir Leekalot..." Timmy panted.

Timmy clenched his teeth and squeezed his eyes shut...

"Gawds almighty, never before have my man tits been worked over in such a fashion Sir Leekalot..." Timmy screeched. "H-how long have we been at this now Sir?"

"Not long enough for me Mr. Bockman, as I say earlier, I can squeeze and mash tits all day..." Sir Leekalot laughed. "All morning, to answer question you just asked, we have been at it all morning..."

Sticking out of the fly opening of his boxer briefs Timmy's hard cock twitched and tried to fuck the air...

"Very soon, very soon I will drink from you again Mr. Bockman..." the Japanese businessman said, sounding very sexy.

"It, its Backman...with an..." Timmy began.

"Yes, with an A, not an O..." Sir Leekalot said into Timmy's ear and nipped gently at his earlobe.

"Well, after all of this tit work and milkin' me I'm really hoping to see a hefty donation here Sir Leekalot..." Timmy panted. "I am workin' hard for you here Sir...AWWWWWWWHH!"

"Donation is in the bag Mr. Bockman with the A," Sir Leekalot said and squeezed the hell out of Timmy's nipples.

"AWWWWWWWW!" Timmy cried out and his cock responded by dribbling a large dollop of pre cum. "I-I have to wonder though if I'll be able to feed you another load of man juice Sir Leekalot...After cummin' twice already that may be a bit of a chore you see..."

"Not to worry Mr. Bockman with the A, I have way to help you shoot the third charm of a load..." Sir Leekalot said and slid his tongue sleazily along the side of Timmy's face.

"AAAAAAHHHHHH...m-my man tits...they sure are numb..." Timmy panted and glanced down at his hard cock, a slight look of mischief on his handsome face. "Wh-what's your plan Sir Leekalot? To make me squirt a third load it's goin' to take some doin' here..."

At that, Sir Leekalot released his hold on Timmy's nipples, grabbed the handsome executive by his hips and spun him around facing forward on his desk... Timmy spun on his cotton briefs covered bottom and then his socked feet were dangling off his desk as Sir Leekalot ran his palms over them...

"Your feet are very sweaty in your socks Mr. Bockman..." the Japanese businessman said.

"Y-yeah, I-I suppose it's safe to say that after what you've been doin' to me here you really got me sweatin' it up in my socks...my word..." Timmy huffed and looked down at his bloated nipples.

"Now Mr. Bockman, you will see how I plan to extract third charmed load from you..." Leekalot drawled and gave Timmy's hard manhood a squeeze. "Or, as you American businessmen say, to be more precise, you won't see..."

Sir Leekalot then held up Timmy's silk necktie...

"Ah dang it all," Timmy seethed as Sir Leekalot reached up and tied Timmy's necktie over his eyes, blindfolding the laddy.

"Now Mr. Bockman, you are to grab your own man tits and squeeze, twist and pinch them till I make you cum third time...the charmed time..." Sir Leekalot said and took Timmy's balls gently in one hand, squeezing them.

"Y-you want me to tweak my own danged tits?" Timmy asked breathlessly and wriggled his toes under his socks.

"Very good way of putting it Mr. Bockman, very precise..." Sir Leekalot said and slurped Timmy's pre cum dribbling cock into his mouth.

"Ahhhhhhhhhh..." Timmy gasped and without another word reached up and did as he had been told, namely, he grabbed his man tits in his fingers and thumbs. "OH GAWDS, my man tits feel so alien to me Sir Leekalot. They have never been so jutted up and hard before...n-no wonder you blindfolded me for this...this way I can really feel the texture of my newly formed nubs..."

Timmy panted and bucked up and down on his desktop as Sir Leekalot chugged his cock down deep into his throat. He teased the laddy by swirling his tongue over and over the crown of Timmy's cock and then gulping his entire girth back down his throat.

"OHHHHHHH FUCKING fucks..." Timmy grunted throatily and looked up at the ceiling with his blindfolded eyes.

His hard cock churned with a life of it's own in the Japanese businessman's mouth...

Sir Leekalot sucked Timmy harder and harder with each passing second...

Timmy tweaked and twisted his nipples, sending chills and thrills through his very being...

"OHHHHHHHHHH...I-I'm getting close now Sir Leekalot...I'm dribbling more than a leaky faucet..." Timmy said with a grin.

"Yes, like my wife Makya told me, you do leak a lot..." Sir Leekalot said and quickly slurped Timmy back into his mouth.

"Y-your wife Makya?" Timmy drawled and suddenly he knew where he had heard the name Leekalot before.

But before Timmy could recall that entire day in Valerie's office when he had once more become a captive in the "Spinning Chinaman" he shot his third (and charmed) load gushing and spewing down Sir Leekalot's craw...

"AAARRRRHHHH GAWD, I-I'm harder than concrete and spewin' like a danged jet engine..." Timmy seethed and thrust himself upwards on his rear end as he sent gulps upon gulps of his cock juice down Sir Leekalot's throat. "Leekalot, dang, fucking Makya, Makya Leekalot..."

Had Timmy not been blindfolded he would have seen the

mischievous looking smile playing on Sir Leekalot's face as he chugged down Timmy's goop... The Japanese businessman tugged on Timmy's balls and Timmy spewed another good glob of his man juices...

"OHHHHHRRRRR fucking controllin' my cock with my balls eh Sir Leekalot?" Timmy grunted breathlessly.

A few moments later, when Timmy had no more good stuff to feed his office guest, Sir Leekalot let the handsome laddy's cock slip slowly from his mouth, swirling his tongue around and around it as he went, sending chills and thrills through Timmy...

"Ah, Mr. Bockman, you are good businessman, very good businessman indeed, I chose well with you last night, as did Bull," Sir Leekalot said as Timmy sat on his desk facing forward, panting in ecstasy and reached up to take the blindfold off himself, leaving it dangling around his neck.

Sir Leekalot reached up as well, to give Timmy's puffed up and very sensitive nipples a few last squeezes and twists...

"Okay Sir Leekalot, I've fulfilled my end of this deal here," Timmy said with authority now in his voice. "Now you can fulfill yours...my vice president is waiting...and you and I need to get some lunch. It sure was a long morning..."

"Yes, it certainly was long morning at that Mr. Backman..." Leekalot said.

"Well, well, Backman with an A, not Bockman with an O," Timmy laughed.

Sir Leekalot smiled upward at Timmy, snapped the elastic in his black socks and reached into his suit jacket pocket for his checkbook... While Sir Leekalot wrote a check in the area of *very* high numbers Timmy hopped down off his desk and padded on socked feet over to the chair where his suit and undershirt had been piled up. As he reached for his tee shirt he heard Sir Leekalot say, "No, no, not so fast Mr. Backman...as you just says, you and I need to have lunch..."

"Yeah, so?" Timmy asked, standing next the office chair with his hand dangling just over his clothes.

"So *you* will eat later, *I* plan to eat now..." the Japanese businessman said and pointed a twitching finger at Timmy's chest, or, to be more precise at his much jutted up nipples.

Timmy pursed his lips together and stifled a gulp...

"Oh my word..." Timmy whispered and he felt his nipples tingle.

"Yes Mr. Backman with no O, man tits are the specialty on the lunch menu I think..." Sir Leekalot said with a grin.

A few moments later Timmy was standing at attention against a wall in his office. His hands had been tethered behind him at the wrists with packaging tape that he'd had in his desk drawer and as he stood there docile, still in just his white boxer briefs and black socks Sir Leekalot feasted alternately on the handsome laddy's nipples. The Japanese man sucked and slurped heartily on Timmy's right nipple and tweaked the other one with his fingers and thumb, mashing it hard. Then he sucked Timmy's left nipple and tweaked and meanly pinched the other one with his fingers and thumb.

"OOOOOOOOO..." Timmy swooned, his head slightly spinning as he glanced over at the huge check that Sir Leekalot had written as it lay on his desk. "L-like I've said all the live long day Sir Leekalot; you sure do love my danged man tits..."

Timmy's sore cock was, unbelievably, at half mast in his boxer briefs...

"My word, but my big ol' man tits are going to be sucked up to epic proportions..." the handsome laddy commented and he smiled snidely over at his desk as he continued to take in the sight of the huge check he had garnered for the bank. "Just not sure why you insisted on taping my hands up behind me...but like I said, it's all for the cause right?"

"Yes, sucked up to epic proportions and then some Mr. Bockman, I mean Backman, with no O but an A, ha, ha..." Sir Leekalot said. "And for good cause it is that your hands are now taped behind you Mr. Backman... a very good cause indeed..."

That said the Japanese businessman stopped sucking Timmy's nipples, pointed a twitching finger at his chest and bulbuous nipples and said, "Please not to move Mr. Backman..."

Timmy watched and then his chin dropped down and his mouth opened wide in sheer terror when he saw Sir Leekalot take two long chopsticks out of his attaché case. To further Timmy's horror he saw that at the ends of the chopsticks were short pointy feathers.

"Oh no, no, wh-what are those for Sir Leekalot?" Timmy bantered as the man stepped back over to him.

"In honor of last nights wonderful fundraiser and all the money that was made I am going to give you what you Americans call a taste of what you experienced there...yes Mr. Backman with no O?" Sir Leekalot asked Timmy. "Let's make you laugh some yes Mr. Backman?"

"Oh no, no, not necessary Sir Leekalot, most definitely not necessary..." Timmy pleaded as Sir Leekalot held his chopsticks under one arm and tied the laddy's tie back over his eyes, blindfolding him. "OH dang it all, please don't do this to me Sir Leekalot, you don't know what it'll do to me..."

"Oh but I do know what it will do to you Mr. Backman with no O, I do know," Sir Leekalot chuckled as he fiddled with Timmy's underpants, sliding them down his legs and off him. "It is going to tickle you Mr. Backman, Mr. Ticklish Laddy..."

"HOO, HOO, HOO, HOO, HOO, HOO, HOO, Ha, ha, ha, ha, ha, ha, ha, ha, ha, ha, ha!" was the sound that Timmy made a few moments later as he stood hands tied and blindfolded as Sir Leekalot tickled his man tits with the feathered chopsticks.

Timmy danced stupidly against the wall in just his black socks as Sir Leekalot stood in front of him. With one hand he tickled Timmy's nipples with the chopsticks; with the other hand he slowly stroked Timmy's now sorely hard cock...

"Third time was the charm Mr. Backman, what shall we call fourth time?" Sir Leekalot asked his laughing and dancing prey.

"M-misery, ha, ha, ha, ha, ha, ha, ha, ha, ha, ha, ha, for poor me it's going to be called misery...HAHAHAHAHAHAHAHAHA!" Timmy said as tears of laughter formed behind his blindfold.

The Bound and Gagged Dishwasher Boy

"RRRRMMMMMMffffff!" the lanky and well muscled Spanish stud roared angrily with his head craned back and watching miserably as my buddy Leo slid his hard steel-like cock into his sweet hole and began fucking him good and hard, reaming the tar out of him to be totally fucking precise.

"Oh yeah, feels real fucking good in this hole of his man!" Leo said to me breathlessly as the rest of us stood around with our hard cocks hanging out of our pants. "Nice and tight, real squishy in there too, better than a goddamned woman's pussy! God almighty, this kid's hole is literally sucking my cock deeper and deeper into it."

"RRRRRRMMMMffffff!" the Spanish stud complained bitterly behind his gag and pulled hard like a madman on the ropes binding him to the table I had lashed him to.

"Yeah, I know bud, you're loving every minute of this," I said teasingly to the bound up stud as he looked at me through his now tear filled eyes. "Shit, I would bet that you're wondering why you're so lucky and what you did to deserve all of this!"

All totaled (and to the Spanish stud's dismay I might add) there were six of us there, taking turns fucking the guy repeatedly. Leo, a muscular guy with dark hair and dark eyes was at the moment enjoying the fruits of the bound and gagged dishwasher that I had snagged for all of us that night. Bruce, Leo's CO-worker was standing nearby waiting his turn to have at the delectable dishwasher as he writhed miserably and helplessly in the tight bondage I had tied him in. Bruce is as muscular and well built as Leo is with lighter brown hair and dark eyes. Wayne, a buddy of mine with wavy black hair and a beard who was in town visiting relatives was awaiting his turn at the sweet treat spread out before all of us. The studly dishwasher was a feast lashed to the table for all of us to enjoy that night. My two buddies Alex and Ronald, the biggest practical jokers in the world had already had their way with the Spanish guy with the short-cropped black hair and thin mustache. Alex is a lanky blond guy who delights in playing mean jokes on people and just making their lives miserable. The scene in front of us was right up his twisted alley. Ronald, a muscular guy built somewhat like a bull had already fucked the trapped dishwasher with his fat beefy cock. Ronald is a dopey looking guy with short brown hair. Lastly, besides yours truly being there was my good buddy Dexter. Dexter is a handsome Asian guy who I've known for a lot of years. Like me, he has one of the biggest cocks on the planet and more than a few times in the past we've enjoyed scenes like this one that I'm now describing to you. We were all having a grand old time, waiting our turns to fuck the poor trapped dishwasher guy. We were all having fun that is except for the poor fuck that I'd volunteered to be our pussy boy that night. Some of us as I said were waiting for seconds and even third goes at his suffering tight hole. Fuck, I had fucked him more than a couple of times myself before calling my buddies and getting them there and I knew that some of them would definitely go for more rounds with his guy's hot hole.

"Shit man, this kid's hole is real fucking hot," my buddy Alex who had already fucked the guy said while standing next to me. "Where'd you get him and how did you get him into the position he's in?"

I smiled and took a long pull on my cigarette.

"Well Alex, if you really want to know I'll tell you," I replied and clamped a hand on Alex's shoulder.

The bound and gagged dishwasher looked up at me again with eyes filled with hatred and death.

"RRRRRRMMMFFFFF!" he roared insanely as his asshole was plowed and we used him like a cheap whore.

My name is Rocco, Rocco Barone to be exact. It had been a

long and grueling night on the night shift where I was stationed by the construction company that I work for. We had just spent from four PM till one AM starting a renovation job in a hallway in a skyscraper in downtown Manhattan. I was fucking dog-tired and to put it plainly I had a boner the size of a python in my scuffed and sweat soaked jeans. Working all day slinging hammers and sweating like a goddamned pig makes me hornier than a bitch in heat on a hot summer night. On the way home in my van I decided to stop and have a bite to eat at what I thought was an all night diner not too far from my neighborhood. I also figured that I could pick up some hot pussy action at the diner as well. At that time of the night there was always some action waiting to be plucked at the diner, whether it be a lonely bitch whose boyfriend had just dumped her, a wife whose husband was out cheating on her, or maybe just a horny tight assed waitress looking for a good fuck from a sleazy stud like me. Little did I know at that moment just how very fucking lucky I was going to get that night. When I pulled into the deserted parking lot it was around two AM. As I pulled my big van into the parking lot I saw the Spanish dishwasher guy locking the door of the diner. He had his back to me and he was clad in the traditional white dishwasher uniform of tight trousers rolled up at the bottom over his black heat and water soaked ankle length boots and his white cotton collared shirt. He was illuminated in my headlights and to put it plainly the sight of his tight small butt in those white pants sent me into a tailspin. The way his sweet cheeks were outlined made me gulp real hard and a mean sinister feeling enveloped me bud. I had always been what's called a real "ladies man", but fuck, the guy's butt looked good enough to fucking eat in those tight white pants of his. And, horny as I was I was not above using the stud to satisfy my lusty and filthy passions. "Looks like it's my lucky night," I murmured to myself as the guy turned around, pocketing the keys.

He had a scar pocked face, but somehow handsome still the same. I guessed that he'd been in numerous fights, no doubt over some pretty senorita. I chuckled at the thought of that and thinking how I was going to turn him into a pussy boy, my own personal senorita. His skin was olive complexion and he had deep and intense looking dark eyes. Fuck, he had a look in his eyes that was equal to the one in mine. I could see that his body was well-toned; doubtless from all the dishes he'd washed and heaved over his time working at the diner. Carrying stacks of washed glass dishes will put muscles on a stud after a good length of time that's for sure. His shirt buttons were open at the top and the upper part of his smooth chest was exposed. My boner pounded at the thought of his pretty doubtless to be brown pointy nipples. Somehow I got the feeling that the stud dishwasher had nipples fat as a woman's, and man, do I love chewing and sucking a good pair of tits let me tell you. He was a bit sweaty looking. I imagined him standing in front of a huge tub-like sink for hours, running hot water, sweating in his boots as he washed and washed and washed dirty dishes. As he started to walk toward the only other car in the parking lot I beeped my horn at him and leaned my head slightly out the window.

"Hey there Pedro, what's going on?" I called out to him.

He stopped walking and looked over at me, pointing at himself.

"Yeah you, I thought this was an all night diner," I said.

"My name is not Pedro Sir," he said, sounding slightly angered as he made his way (stupidly) over to me, also speaking with a slight Spanish accent. "Eet's Miguel. And no, thees is no longer an all night diner."

His Spanish accent made him all the more alluring for some reason. The intense look in his eyes made me want to wipe that smirk off his face in the worst possible fashion. I waited till he was standing directly in front of my driver's side window.

"When did they stop being an all night diner Pedro?" I asked him with a sneer, taking a look around to make sure there was no chance whatsoever of being seen what I was about to do.

"As I said Meester, my name is not Pedro," he said again, this time through clenched teeth.

Obviously he didn't appreciate my Spanish humor.

"And they stopped being an all night diner about two months ago," he went on. "There wasn't enough business to keep the place open all night. "Gosh darn it all," I said, trying to sound as stupid as possible as I sat peering at him, taking in the sight and scent of him all at the same time.

He smelled of a mixture of dishwater, dish detergent, and sweat, the sweat of a real hard worker. I guessed his height to be around five feet six inches tall, real short to my six foot plus gait. Short as he was though he had the look of a real street tough mean guy. And if he couldn't tell that he was being sized up for a real all night fuck-fest than he was dumber than I even thought.

"That shows how long I haven't been here huh?" I asked him, still sounding as stupid as possible as I got my hand slowly out window. "Do you possibly know where there is an all night diner by any chanc--- "

But before I finished my sentence I had my big ham-sized hand out the window and swiftly around his neck.

"ACCCHHHHHH!" the dishwasher squealed suddenly, his eyes bulging in shock in his head as I squeezed his neck hard, squeezing the wind from him. "OH MY GOD!"

"Well Pedro my boy, it looks to me like you've gotten yourself into a bit of trouble here eh?" I asked him jokingly as he splayed his arms uselessly and tottered on his wet booted feet.

He swung his fists but all he succeeded in doing was punching my van… There was no way he could get to my face.

"Wh-what the fuck, *what the fuck are you d-doing Meester?*" he asked in a rage as I pulled him helplessly forward and banged his forehead against the side of my van.

"HHHUUUFFFFF!" he grunted and I held him still very tight by the neck.

Looking at him I saw that his eyes were rolling in incomprehension in their sockets.

"Heh," I chuckled and pulled him forward again by the neck, slamming his forehead again against the side of my van.

"HUUUFFFFFF!" he grunted again miserably. "Ohhhhhh you meeserable fucker!"

"Heh, heh, one more good rap should do it eh Pedro?" I asked him. "The lump you're going to have will look real nice with all those scars of yours."

"M-my name ees Miguel," he said in total confusion and I yanked him forward again.

His head banged meanly against the side of my van a third time, stunning the total fuck out of him. I let go of his neck and he slid to the ground against the side of my van, a dishwasher soaked heap of Spanish stud. Lying there on the ground staring up at the stars he seemed to be wondering what the fuck had just happened. I quickly grabbed some utility rope and hopped out of the van, a mean looking grin on my face spreading from ear to ear…

In what were just a few moments later I had the kid standing next to my van. His sinewy muscular arms were roped tight at his sides against his body, pinned there real securely. The slack of rope was in my hand to be used as a leash. I had crammed an old sweat soaked red bandana of mine into his mouth and slapped a wad of duct tape over it, thoroughly gagging him.

"Like I said Pedro, it sure looks like you've gotten yourself into a bit of trouble here tonight eh?" I asked him snidely, holding onto the rope and yanking him slightly forward on his black booted feet.

"HHHHRRRRRRmmmmfffff!" he sputtered meanly and angrily at me.

The way his eyes were rolling in his head I guessed that the taste of my sweaty bandanna was sickening to him.

"Yeah, yeah, I know, your fucking name is Miguel," I said to him and yanked him even more, forcing him along, almost knocking him off his feet. "So you were the guy whose turn it was to lock up this dump tonight huh?"

That said I pulled him close to me and took the keys to the diner out of his pants pocket, my hand getting a tad too close to his most private region as I rummaged in his pocket a little longer than was necessary.

"RRRRMMMFFFFF!" he sputtered, looking at me with eyes that were obviously filled with thoughts of me robbing the diner.

Fuck it all, nothing could have been further from the truth. This poor fuck had no clue yet as to just what the hell I had in mind for him. And that is exactly what it would be for him, hell, *total fucking hell.*

"Were you just headed home Pedro?" I asked him, sounding totally mocking, noticing the wedding band on his left ring finger. "Got a pretty wife waiting for you to ram her pussy for her buddy boy? Well, your plans for the evening have just been altered, very altered."

I slid his wedding band off his ring finger and he squealed like a banshee behind his gag as I did so.

"You're my wife now Pedro," I said to him meanly.

I pocketed the keys and his wedding band and then ripped the topmost part of his open shirt open a little more, revealing those two brown pointy nipples that I was expecting to see.

"Oh yes, nice Pedro, very fucking nice," I exclaimed and tweaked and twirled his nipples hard, twisting them meanly at the same time. "Nice womanly tits you got here Stud…"

"RRRRRHHHffffff!" he garbled into his foul tasting gag.

"Getting the picture now huh Pedro?" I asked him, looking at him lustfully and gleefully at the same time.

His eyes filled with terror at that point as I really worked his nipples super hard. I squeezed the very bejesus out of them, twisted them meanly some more and pinched the tips of them till he was truly squealing and squawking into his gag. As I pinched the fuck out of the tips of his nips he involuntarily heaved himself up to his tiptoes in his boots and ranted angrily at me, his intense dark eyes filled with total loathing for me. Fuck, by the time the night was over he'd more than loath me that was for sure. I tweaked his nipple tips some more and the poor guy looked down and watched. I got the feeling that he must have been thinking that I was planning to rip his tits right off his chest…

A few minutes later I had tied some rope around the dishwasher's booted feet, leaving a few inches of slack in between them. When made to walk as I pulled on the leash he was doing so clumsily and awkwardly.

"Come on Pedro, lets you and I go back inside the diner and have some fun what do you say?" I asked him as I pulled him along on the leash-like rope.

"HHHRRRRFFFFFF!" he replied and nearly lost his footing.

"Come on you can do it," I said to him snidely. "I have faith in you."

He looked totally helpless and fear filled as I dragged him along to the entrance door of the diner that he had just so recently locked. His nipples were tweaked up nice and pointy on his chest and I swear by all that's holy and all that's not that he had a boner in his white dishwasher uniform pants big enough to choke a goddamned horse with. I guessed my really working his succulent nipples and being in total unabashed terror had gotten him good and fear hard in his pants. When we got to the door of the diner he squealed and grunted angrily into his gag as I tried a few different keys to get the door unlocked.

"Relax Pedro, we'll be in there in a few seconds," I said to him as I slid another key into the lock.

At that moment he tried to bolt away from me on his hobbled feet.

I grinned and simply grabbed the slack of the rope and yanked him back to me.

"HHHRRRRRMMMFFFF!" he protested and then I punched him good and hard across the face, sending him sprawling to the pavement. "GGGRRRRRHHFFFFFF!"

"There, now you got another scar to add to your collection Pedro," I said to him, sounding totally insane, even to myself.

My cock pounded like a jackhammer in my jeans...

I reached down and hauled him back up to his tied feet by his neck, him squealing and screaming into his gag at that point... Obviously the stud knew what he was in for...

"Try that shit again you little piece of shit and you'll be sorrier than ever before in your life," I said threateningly to him, letting go of his neck.

His eyes filled with tears and I smiled wickedly at him. I pecked his gagged mouth and in a split second I hoisted him off the ground and under one huge muscular arm.

"RRRMMMFFFF!" Miguel grunted as I got the door of the diner open and carried him in an upside down U shaped position into the establishment.

His wet boots dripped on the floor as I lugged him to the center of the somewhat elegant looking dining room. When I passed right by the cash register he grunted in confusion, but when I slammed him down atop a table in the dining room on his stomach I think was when he really started to figure it out. The way he looked around the deserted dining room told me that his head was still spinning from the blows I had dealt him.

"RRRMMMFFFF!" he screamed as I turned on one light, just enough for me to see what I would be getting that night.

He was lying there on his stomach like a stuck pig atop that table. I quickly untied his feet, breathing in the scent of his wet boots and spread his legs apart, making them dangle real sexily off the sides of the table.

"Keep your legs just as I've positioned them you little shit," I said to him. "Fucking do as I say or you're really going to know what the fuck trouble is." Again his eyes filled with tears. I stood menacingly over him and drank in the sight of him lying there; I drank in the sight of him as a vampire would drink the blood of a choice victim. The dishwasher boy's tight white pants were hugging his exquisite butt cheeks like they were in love with them, it looked to me like his pants loved hugging those butt cheeks of his and I could see the outline of his underpants through them.

"Oh Pedro, what a fucking sight you are to behold," I said to him, taking a pair of heavy-duty scissors off my utility belt. "Now, don't move pussy boy."

I carefully began cutting away the backside portion of the kid's uniform pants, the edge of the scissors running along his sexy underpants under them. My breath came in short gasps as I did my work. A few minutes later I had the dishwasher's backside of his pants cut away and I meanly ripped away his white underpants. What was revealed was one of the sexiest girlie asses I had ever seen in my life. Miguel had small tight ass cheeks the likes of two globes or melons. They were tight enough to bounce a quarter off. Shaking in ecstasy I took a handful of one of them and gave it a hard squeeze.

"RRRRMMMFFFFFF!" the kid garbled in disbelief.

"Heh, heh, no doubt you're straight huh Pedro?" I asked him teasingly and grabbed his other ass cheek. Oh yeah, fuck it all boy so am I, so am I. Your wedding band tells me so in your case. Fuck, straight as I am this ass of yours has to be the sweetest and sexiest thing I've seen in a long fucking time."

With that and with his ass cheeks in hands I pulled the melon shaped globes apart, revealing a pink, moist gaping pussy hole.

"Oh fuck, oh good God, better than a woman's pussy you little shit," I panted and leaned down. "What a waste that this pussy hole should be attached to a stud like you. Bet your woman loves to squeeze the fuck out of your sexy sweet cheeks while you fuck her silly huh Pedro?"

He reeled madly on the table as, like a dog, I sniffed greedily at his hole, flicking my tongue over it a few times; I drooled in it and then sucked up my saliva real greedily. The kid squealed in total anger and violation. I squeezed his ass cheeks good and fucking hard as I tongued and feasted and sniffed at his hole. It smelled raw and funky deep in there with just a trace of shit mixed in. I figured he must have taken a dump recently. But how that sweet hole twitched every time I pressed my tongue against it bud, like it had a life of its own let me tell you. Miguel squirmed miserably atop the table as I helped myself and tongued and teased his wet hole like crazy.

"Ha, I got the feeling you wash dishes for hours Pedro, your stink hole is just oozing with moisture," I said meanly. "And judging from how wet and sloppy those boots of yours are I'll bet they keep you stashed away in that hot kitchen all fucking day… What a waste…"

I kissed his hole good and hard and sucked it meanly…

"RRHHHFFFFFFF!" the dishwasher ranted.

Reaching further between his splayed legs I found his hairy sweaty sexy sac and gave it a few squeezes, really getting the guy grunting meanly into his gag.

"Okay Pedro my pussy boy, what say we get this show on the road huh?" I asked him and dashed over to the serving counter. "Don't go anywhere now, heh, heh."

I kept an eye on him as I found just what the fuck I was looking for under the take-out area of the serving counter, packaging rope. I quickly dashed back over to my pussy boy and got to work on really securing him to the tabletop. Man oh man did he grunt and squirm atop that table while I worked at roping him tightly down to it. When I was done his legs were spread more than wide and his backside was hanging just off the end of the table, his sweet stink hole a ready target for what I was going to be feeding it real soon. His booted ankles were tied off to the legs of other nearby heavy tables, keeping his hole good and fucking visible. His upper body was roped down tight, almost in a spider web conglomeration fashion, pinning him to the tabletop.

"Man, if your wife could see you now Pedro," I said to him, fingering his wedding band in my pocket.

He lifted his head up off the table and roared maniacally at me through his gag.

"But like I said before, you're my wife now," I said and unhooked my belt.

His eyes opened wider and wider in total fear, knowing all too well what he was in for.

"Ha, got it all figured out already huh Pedro?" I asked him as I shucked my filthy jeans down around my ankles along with my grungy and stinking piss stained underpants. "I should have blindfolded you as well. Now, get ready."

My meat stick is of the jumbo-sized bud let me tell you. Any woman

I've ever been with has screamed bloody ecstasy as I plowed her with it. This was one of those special times that my big guy would be spearing a male asshole. My balls hung big and plump in my hairy sac and I entered the tied and gagged dishwasher boy inch by painful inch.

"OHHHHHHRRRR FUCK, it's warmer and tighter than a pussy in there Pedro," I grunted truthfully. "OHHHHRRRR shit, I may just switch to guys full time."

I again grabbed his exquisite ass cheeks and slid my rod still further inside him.

"HHHRRRRRMMMMMFFF!" he squealed as his hole stretched to accommodate me.

"OHHHHHHHHHH fucking A you hot pussy boy, fate was kind to me tonight!" I gasped and slid myself the rest of the way inside him.

The kid panted miserably, screaming into his gag and squirmed helplessly in the bondage as I got a good rhythm going, thrusting inside him like crazy, pulling myself only slightly out of him each time. My cock never left his hole for a second. He grunted and garbled crazily and insanely as I fucked him, fucked him, squeezed and kneaded his ass cheeks, fucked him some more and slapped his ass cheeks real fucking hard.

"OHHHHHRRRRR fuck, I can do this all night Pedro," I whispered throatily, thrusting like a madman and slapping his ass cheeks, the sounds of the slaps resounding in the deserted diner.

The sounds of squishing filled the area as well as I slid beautifully in and out and in and out of his hole.

"OHHHHHHRRRR God, I'm getting close man, I am going to shoot a fucking load like never before in my life," I said huskily.

And with that I let fly with a mess of slop to rival no other in my life. At the tender age of thirty-three I was spewing a mess the likes of that of a seventeen year old.

"OHHHHHHRRRR yeah, yeah, fucking awesome man!" I seethed and squeezed the fuck out of Miguel's luscious ass cheeks, filling his hole liberally with my construction worker juices.

When I was done I let my slimy piece slide slowly out of his stink hole. It came out and Miguel farted. I laughed meanly, took a half-smoked cigar from my shirt pocket and fired it up. The smell of my cigar drowned out the smell of Miguel's fart.

"Give me a few minutes man and I'll be back inside you again with a vengeance like you won't believe," I said to him, puffed my cigar and slid a couple of fingers deep inside the kid's now sopping wet hole.

He heaved horribly on the table and there were huge tears streaming down his scar pocked face…

It was ten minutes later and I was again plowing the kid's hole. Standing there smoking my cigar with two fingers jammed in the kid's silky warm hole had gotten me hard all over again let me tell you. With my cigar smoldering in my mouth I fucked and fucked and fucked that dishwasher with every fucking thing I had. I held tightly to his twitching butt cheeks and slammed myself in and out of him like crazy. By now he was a sweaty and stinking mess atop that table. With each thrust his hole became moister and more delectable. This time when I filled his hole with my juices I took my cigar out of my mouth, put it down by his tear streaked face and buried my mouth against his sopping hole. I sucked my juices out of his hole along with his funky scent and gulped it all down. A few minutes of that and I was hard again, unbelievably. When I slid into him the third time his head came up off the table in total disbelief.

"Yeah, ohhhhh yeah, like I told you Pussy boy, I can do this all night long," I grunted and gyrated my hips as I fucked him and fucked him and fucked him. "Women absolutely adore me man that I can fuck all night long! But you Pedro, I'll just bet a week's salary that you hate me like no one else ever before in your life. Ohhhhhhh fuck, oh yeah! Best hole my cock has been inside of in a long fucking while."

A little while later, after having fucked him more than a few times I sat down at a table nearby the trussed up dishwasher.

"What a night it turned out to be huh Pedro?" I asked him, my long legs stretched out in front of me.

I shucked off my boots and got my jeans and underpants off me as well. That would give me more freedom of movement the next time I reamed the dishwasher's hole.

"I'll bet your wife is wondering where the fuck you are huh Pedro?" I said and took a fresh cigar from my shirt pocket, slid it into my mouth and fired it up. "You got kids?"

He nodded "yes" and cried some more, no doubt from the pain his sweet hole was feeling.

"Kind of young to have kids, you don't look anymore than twenty or so," I said and laughed meanly.

He turned his face away from me and I sat there enjoying my cigar, wallowing in the sight of him all trussed up and pinned down to that table. When my cigar was halfway smoked I walked over to the bar and picked up a bottle of scotch and a small funnel.

"How about a drink Pedro?" I asked him from the bar and he turned to look at me.

When he saw me holding up the bottle of scotch and the funnel he screamed crazily into his gag, spittle flying from the sides of his gagged mouth.

"Fuck it all man, I am sure glad I got you gagged," I said in a silly tone as I approached him. "If not you'd be waking up the whole neighborhood. Fuck man, you act as though you've never been the main course at a fuck buffet before Pedro."

Without any warning I slid the stem of the funnel into Miguel's well-fucked asshole.

"MMMMFFFF!" he gasped loudly at the invasive funnel.

I slid it further into him, wedging it in, teasing his poor hole with it as I did the task…

"Okay, this will have you flying and begging for more fucking very soon Pedro," I said to him and poured scotch slowly through the stem of the funnel and into the kid's asshole.

"HHHRRRRRMMMFFFF!" the dishwasher gasped and I could tell from his eyes that his head was spinning in no time.

"Yeah, that stuff kicks in real fast eh Pedro?" I asked him mockingly. "And from the end that you're drinking it from you'll be sloshed before you can even think of how to spell your name. Nothing like a good scotch every once in a while…"

I poured a goodly amount of the scotch into him, set the bottle aside and once again slid my boner into his hole.

"ARRRRRRhhhhhh yeah, fucking A you hot bitch!" I ranted as my hard-on thrust deep into him. "Fucking hotter bitch than a woman you are you fucking stud!"

Miguel's hole was squishy and awash with his stinking shit sweat, my cum and now the scotch too. The three scents combined drove me to higher heights and I fucked him insanely. His head spun away and he cried pitifully as I rammed him harder and harder.

"No more tough guy huh Pedro?" I teased him, slapping his creamy white ass cheeks as I fucked him and fucked him. "Bet those guys you were in street fights with would love to see you now huh? Fuck, fuck, I made you into my goddamned bitch you studly bastard!"

This time it really took me a while to pop my load, but no big deal bud; I was having a grand old time fucking the tar out of the hotter than hot Spanish guy. His tight hole felt as if it were literally sucking my hard cock into and out of it.

It was way beyond fifteen minutes later when I exploded my juices for the umpteenth time inside the trussed up kid. Standing there in my stinking white sweat socks and my ratty tee shirt and stinking of hot and rancid construction worker sweat I popped a good squirt into my captive.

"OHHHHHHHRRRRR GOD," I screeched through clenched teeth, my eyes squeezed shut. "OHHHHHHRRRR fuuuccckkkk, I've cum so many damned times that it's actually starting to hurt Pedro!"

With my rod still inside him I grabbed his succulent ass cheeks real hard and jiggled them meanly...

When I was done this time I really needed to relax in order to get my juices flowing again. Sitting at the nearby table I smoked what was left of my cigar as my cock hung all slimy and semi hard between my legs. On the table I had the bottle of scotch *and* my cell phone.

"What a night this is huh Pedro?" I asked him again with a grin and puffed on my cigar, swigging down gulps of scotch in between. "And guess what?"

At that question he managed to lift his head up off the table and look miserably over at me. He was punch drunk on the scotch I had fed into his asshole, ha! Judging from the look in his eyes he was hurting like never before in his life. His handsome scar pocked face was streaked with tears and he was trembling violently under the ropes.

"I think I'll call a few of my good buddies to really get this party going," I said, picking up my cell phone. "What do you say huh? Something as hot and fresh as you should be shared I think. Selfish of me to just fuck you all night long by myself and not share the wealth."

"HHHHRRRRRmmmmmmffff!" he squealed insanely into his gag,

knowing exactly what the fuck he was in for now.

"Yeah, I know, you're wondering what the fuck you did to deserve all this," I said as I dialed my buddy Leo's number.

He picked up on the second ring.

"Fuck hello, this better be a fire," Leo said into the phone, more asleep than awake.

"Hey Leo, its Rocco, listen, have I got a fucking treat for you man," I said gleefully. "Wake Bruce up, get some clothes on and get over to the Moon Rise and Shine Diner on King Street, pronto!"

"Rocco, what the fuck are you talking about man?" Leo asked me, sounding very confused. "The Moon Rise and Shine is closed at this time of night."

"Not to us it ain't," I said and held the phone in the air.

"HHHRRRRRMMFFFFF!" Miguel roared, stupidly letting his presence be known.

"Oh fuck Rocco, I don't know what the hell you've got there but we're on our way buddy," Leo said and hung up.

Snickering now I dialed my buddy Alex's number. Miguel cried and screamed in outright terror behind his gag…

Overall I had called six of my most sadistic and kinky buddies. Alex and Ronald arrived first. I saw their car pull up in the parking lot of the place and the headlights were quickly doused. I dashed to open the door for them, still wearing just my tee shirt and sweat socks.

"Fuck man, check you out in all your fucking semi naked glory," Alex said, gave my slimy cock a tug and smiled at me as he and Ronald came into the diner. "Shit, not to mention that you smell real raunchy and sexy too Rocco."

"Yeah and here's the reason why," I said as I led them over to where Miguel was.

"H-h-holy fucking shit man!" Alex squealed happily and jumped up and down like a school kid in delight. "Where in the fuck did you get this piece of ass?"

Both of them smiling meanly Alex and Ronald stepped behind the trussed up Spanish guy and began stealing squeezes on his hot, hot ass cheeks.

"Shit man Rocco, he's a he," Ronald said, looking over at me in utter confusion. "I thought you'd gotten your hands on some real hot pussy gal."

"Oh he's a real hot pussy gal Ronald, trust me on that buddy," I said and took a long swig of scotch.

"Look man, I'm no faggot," Ronald went on.

"Ha, neither am I man, but I've been fucking the tar out of that sweet hole for more than an hour or so now," I said meanly. "And believe you me, it feels tighter than a pussy in there."

But suddenly our conversation was cut short because it was at that moment that Alex had lowered his jeans and underpants and slid his hard-on into Miguel's hole.

"RRRMMMMFFFF!" Miguel sputtered madly, causing Ronald and I to stop our conversation, us talking about Miguel as if he weren't even there, as if he weren't even a person.

"Ohhhhh fuck man Ronald, Rocco is right, this kid's hole is as tight as a drum and squishy as any pussy I've ever had the good fortune to fuck," Alex panted as he slid his hardness deeply in and back out of Miguel's hole over and over and over again. "Ohhhhhrrr fuck, I get the feeling we'll be here all night for this."

"Only till about five thirty AM bud," I said with caution in my voice. "This place opens at six."

"Then we'll have to fuck him good but fast," Alex said and smacked Miguel's ass cheeks a good and stinging blow.

"HHRRRRMMMFFFFF!" Miguel gasped.

While Alex was busy spearing the kid's hole I saw more headlights in the parking lot as Leo and Bruce arrived next. I dashed over to the door to let them in once they were out of their car.

"Ohhhhhhhrrr shit man Ronald, I can fuck this tight hole all night long," Alex heaved heartily and buried his cock deeper and deeper inside the kid with each thrust.

Like Alex and Ronald before them Leo and Bruce could not believe the scene being played out in front of them as I walked them into the diner. Leo was holding my scmi hard cock in his hand as we walked into the dining room.

"Fuck man, your cock is all slimy and sore feeling," Leo quipped jokingly. "It feels like you've been busy fucking the tar out of this guy over and over."

"That I have," I replied as Leo gave my cock a few tugs.

Leo and Bruce claim they're straight but I seriously doubt it. I mean, its been more than a few times that Leo has had my manhood in his hand. Wayne arrived by himself a little while later after Leo and Bruce and Dexter, as always was tardy. After Alex had popped his load wildly into the kid's hole Ronald wasted no time slamming his very fat cock into him next.

"RRRRMMMFFFFF!" the tied down Spanish guy screamed in agony into his gag.

Looking around at my buddies with their boners hanging out of their pants and me just about stark fucking naked Miguel knew in his misery that it was going to indeed be a long night.

"Goddamn it Rocco, just look at the fucking melon shaped butt cheeks this stud has," Wayne commented and squeezed one of Miguel's ass cheeks hard as Ronald speared him madly.

Ronald was breathless and didn't utter a word as he worked his fat cock in and out of the poor trussed up pussy boy.

"Yeah Wayne, it was those hot butt cheeks of his that made me decide to make him our pussy boy for tonight," I replied. "Fuck man, I bet this guy never once in his wildest imaginings thought of himself as a pussy boy for a bunch of twisted gang bangers the likes of us."

At that comment we all guffawed loudly and then for the first time since thrusting his fat tool into Miguel's hole Ronald spoke, breathlessly, but spoke still the same.

"Uhhhhnnnnn ohhhhrrrr God, I-I'm going to pop my big fat nut you guys!" Ronald panted. "OHHHHHRRRRR FUCK, pussy boy here is making me and my cock crazy. OHHHHHHHH fucking A!"

Ronald and Wayne slapped Miguel's ass cheeks real hard and loudly as Ronald squirted his juices deep inside him. Miguel reeled and squirmed angrily and bitterly under the binding tight ropes. He looked up at me with death now showing in his eyes, my death to be exact, as I stood next to the table he was atop of.

"Man oh man Kid, you should see yourself," I quipped at him and ruffled his sweat soaked hair. "Trust me on this, if you saw yourself all tied up the way I got you, you would want to fuck you too."

"HHHRRRMMMFFFF!" he screamed loudly as Ronald's cock slid out of him and Wayne eagerly entered him next. "RRRMMMFFFFF!"

"No rest for the weary huh Pedro?" I asked him snidely.

"Oh man, oh fucking fuck, what a squishy and tight hole," Wayne garbled in ecstasy. "I *know* I'm going to want seconds and thirds at this guy's hole. Fuck man, straight as I am this kid's tight hole is too much to be believed."

Watching as my buddies took their turns spearing and fucking the tar out of the captured dishwasher had my own cock hard as a rock again and wanting to pop another load or a few. Watching a woman get it from a bunch of guys always floated my boat and I guess that watching a guy get it in the same fashion was having the same effect. Deciding not to let the pleasurable feeling pass me by I decided on the other end of the dishwasher. I took the wad of duct tape off his mouth and took the end of the old bandanna rag in his mouth between my thumb and first fingers.

"I'm going to take the gag out of your mouth Pedro," I said to him threateningly. "But I don't want to hear any prattle that you have to say. You see, I'm in need of your mouth at the moment."

That said I wagged my boner in the kid's face and pulled the rag from his mouth. It came out saliva soaked and real chewed up looking. The dishwasher's lips were trembling and he was crying man, crying like fucking crazy. I wondered for all of a second if he would ever be the same after all this. Then I slid my hard cock into his mouth.

"Suck me Pussy boy and if you bight once you're done for," I gasped as his lips closed, seemingly expertly over my throbbing shaft.

Holding him by the top of his head I thrust in and out of the kid's sweet mouth.

"Ohhhhhrrr yeah, we're giving it to him from both ends now," Wayne gasped as he plugged the dishwasher's hole over and over again.

Miguel sucked cock and took it up the ass and cried and squirmed miserably all at once. When Wayne popped his load into the kid's hole I was still enjoying the feeling of his warm mouth, my balls crashing against his chin at the same time he sucked me.

"Looks like you learned to suck cock right fast Pedro," I laughed meanly and Wayne's cock slipped from his hole.

Dexter took position behind the kid and slowly slid his Chinese hardness into him.

Watching the handsome and rugged Chinese guy fuck the mean looking Spanish guy sent my blood rushing through my veins and caused me to pop yet another load.

"OHhhhhhrrrrr yeah, swallow my mess now you fucking hot pussy boy," I garbled loudly, forcing my juices down his gullet.

Dexter meanly slapped the kid's ass cheeks as he plowed him more and more…

Overall we all fucked the kid more than a few times each. Leo was at his second go at the kid's hole while Bruce anxiously awaited his turn…

"And that is how I managed to snag this hot piece of ass for us tonight," I said, answering Alex's question as Leo fucked the dishwasher for the second time, having popped his load and slid his hardness right back in for the second fuck.

I had never known myself or these buddies of mine to shoot their loads and be hard again so soon and so fast; Miguel the dishwasher boy certainly had an effect on us bud…

"Ohhhhhhrrrr yeah, I'm going to cum again," Leo stated, all sweaty and stinking as he held tight to the kid's exquisite butt cheeks and slammed in real deep, stretching the fabric of his hole. "Can't believe it man, I shot two loads one after the other. Ohhhhh yeah!"

"About fucking time," Bruce piped up. "Because it's my turn now."

Miguel looked angrily and maniacally at Bruce through his tear soaked eyes as the guy walked past him and took position at his very open and gaping hole. Cum was dripping freely out of the dishwasher's hole and landing on the floor, we had fucked him that many times. Bruce slid his hardness into the trapped kid and began eagerly pumping away. There was no doubt in my mind that Miguel would feely kill all of us once this was over, given the chance that is. Judging from the look in his eyes we would all be in for it, as I said, given the chance if he had it…

"Ohhhhh fuck Rocco, this feels great," Bruce gasped heavily as his cock slid in and out of the trapped dishwasher's hole.

While Bruce plowed and fucked Miguel's poor hole Dexter took position in front of the kid, ordered him to open wide and then slid his big

Chinese hardness into Miguel's mouth…

"AAARRRRHHH yeah, bet that egg roll of mine tastes real good since it's been way up your shit chute huh Pedro?" Dexter laughed and forced Miguel to deep throat his cock.

By the time it was all over we had all fucked the dishwasher named Miguel more than a few times each. All of our cocks were sore and our balls were drained beyond reason. As we all got dressed, Miguel lay there still tied to the table. His mouth was frothed and crusted with cum and his sweet asshole was dripping and dripping it like crazy.

"F-*fucking maricone, fucking butt pluggers,*" the kid swore under his breath. "You ain't real men if you need to fuck a poor guy like me…"

"You going to take care of getting him untied Rocco?" Leo asked me.

"Sure thing bud," I said, looking over at the bar. "But I think I'll give him one more down the ass hatch, if you know what I mean. Wouldn't want a struggle with him after all this, I just want to get him out of here and on his way."

"Fucking maricone coward," Miguel rasped through clenched teeth. "Fucking untie me now and we'll see just how tough you are bastard!"

After all my buddies were gone I sauntered over to the bar one more time and picked up the bottle of scotch. "Ready for the next round Pedro?" I asked the kid, holding up the bottle and the funnel. "It's on the house after all so you might as well."

"Y-you lowlife scumbag, *YOU FUCKING FAGGOT!*" he spat at me, cum dripping out of his mouth, his lips trembling as he spoke.

With a grin on my face I walked over to him and inserted the stem end of the funnel into his sopping and well-fucked hole.

"UHHHHHFFFF, fucccckkkkk man, I am going to keel you for this shit," Miguel swore as I began pouring the scotch into him rectally. "Ohhhhhhhhh fuuucckkk, m-my poor head feels like it's flying away again…"

This time I gave him more than double the amount of the scotch I'd ass fed him earlier. I wanted the kid beyond sloshed, over the top drunk. I wanted him totally incapable of doing anything when I finally untied him. When I stopped filling him with the scotch he could barely even utter one comprehensible word. I put the scotch back in the bar and deposited the funnel again into the small sink that was filled with soapy water. I quickly dashed back over to the table and began untying Miguel. A few moments later I had him standing next to me on wobbly booted feet. Fuck, he couldn't stand period. I had to hold him up by his upper arms.

"B-bastard," he whispered as he stood there in my grasp with his sexy backside showing out of the back of his dishwasher white pants.

I hoisted him off the floor and slung him over one shoulder…

"Heh, heh, I know just what the fuck to do with you Pedro," I snickered meanly and walked toward the kitchen of the diner, my hand resting on his sweet ass.

At just before opening time at the diner Miguel woke up sitting in the large sink that he washed dishes in day in and day out. I had left him there with the warm water on, soaking his boots and pants. He quickly managed to get his bearings, the scotch having worn off a bit and dashed out of the diner, his backside still fully exposed for the world to see. Checking his pocket he realized that I'd given him back his keys but not his wedding band. He was no doubt thankful that it was still dark outside at that time of the morning as he locked up the diner for the second time, his hands trembling as he fitted the key in the lock. Only this time he was eyeing the parking lot very carefully, making sure that my van wasn't there. Or perhaps he was hoping that my van was there, hell bent on teaching me a lesson for the shit I'd just caused him to suffer. Once the diner was locked up he placed his hands over his exposed ass cheeks and hobbled slowly over to his car. He was obviously still in a lot of pain, seeing as he couldn't walk all that well. He opened the car door and hopped quickly into the driver's seat. Sitting there facing forward with his hands clenched tightly around the steering wheel of the car he slowly and methodically scanned the parking lot, cursing and swearing softly under his breath, his breath coming in slow gasps actually. My van was nowhere in sight. Suddenly, from the right next to him in the passenger seat I grabbed a handful of the top of his hair.

"Wh-what the???" the soaked dishwasher garbled and turned to see me. "H-hoooollyy fuck man!"

He clenched his teeth, said, "I ain't all tied up now Maricone!", but I quickly yanked his head forward, banging his forehead hard against the steering wheel.

"HHHUUFFFFFF!" he gasped as I added yet another new lump to his head.

"Fuck Pedro, it's going to be a long night," I drawled and cackled meanly.

A few minutes later I was driving toward home in my van, the dishwasher trussed up, gagged and blindfolded in the back compartment...

About the Author

Christopher Trevor was born in July 1963 and grew up in New York City. As soon as he was old enough to know how he began writing fiction and has been writing gay erotic/fetish stories for the past ten to twelve years at this point. He became an avid reader as well from the time he knew how and reads everything from fiction, to non-fiction to biographies of interesting and unusual people, people who have made a difference or who have paved the way for others. Christopher attributes his writing artistic inspiration to artists such as Etienne, Tom of Finland, Tagame, The Hun, and most notably Joe T,  who Christopher has had the pleasure of speaking with and even meeting over the last few years. Christopher states, "Joe T encouraged me to write about my fetish because I was embarrassed about it at the time. Joe T said that when we are embarrassed about something that makes it even more enticing somehow." Christopher totally agreed and never stopped writing in this genre. Erotic writers who inspired Christopher Trevor were: Tom Shaw (author of "That Day at the Quarry), C.S. White (author of Big Sur), Larry Townsend (author of countless erotic novels), and Mason Powell (author of the classic story "The Brig.")

Christopher discovered that not only did he enjoy writing erotic tales but that after his first bondage experience he had a genuine flair for it. Writing to erotic oriented magazines about his first bondage experience truly opened the floodgates for Christopher where this style of writing is concerned. Christopher thanks the handsome and muscular "Greg" for that experience way back in time. Christopher took "Creative Writing" courses every semester during his high school years and while other friends of his stopped writing what they loved to write about as time went on Christopher never let a day go by when he didn't write something... "I feel that if I don't write every day I will die," Christopher has said many times over.

Foot fetish stories and all things related; spanking fetish, erotic shaving, muscle bondage, tickle torture, and hardcore stories are just a few of the areas of gay eroticism that Christopher enjoys writing about and inspiring in others as well. As one internet buddy said to Christopher where the black socks fetish is concerned, "Until I started talking with you I never gave a thought to my socks when I got dressed for work in the morning. Now when I pull my dress socks on every morning I get a chill up my spine."

Christopher is proud of the erotic effect he has on people...

Christopher Trevor is also the author of:

The Executive Guide to Foot Fetishism and Office Discipline
1-887895-36-1

Executive Ties That Bind
1-887895-37-X

Don't! Stop! That Tickles!
1-887895-31-0

The Taming of Dominick
1-887895-45-0

Timmy and The Hong Kong Tailor
1-887895-30-2

Love, Torture and Redemption
1-887895-32-9

Timmys Ticklish Trials
978-1-887895-74-3

The Gym Instructor
978-1-887895-44-6

Milked
978-1-887895-66-8

Erotic Street Blues
978-1-887895-97-2

The Abusive Wager
978-1-887895-04-0

Terry's Appointment and Other Tickling Stories
978-1-934625-08-8

The Military File
978-1-934625-21-7

Quirks
978-1-934625-24-8

Look for them where you bought this book or Goodboner.com.

www.ingramcontent.com/pod-product-compliance
Lightning Source LLC
Chambersburg PA
CBHW071221260626
47162CB00004B/1386